DISNEY

DARING
DREAMERS
CLUB

PiPER COOKS UP A PLAN

BY ERIN SODERBERG
ILLUSTRATED BY ANOOSHA SYED

Random House New York

Library of Congress Cataloging-in-Publication Data
Name: Soderberg, Erin, author.
Title: Piper cooks up a plan / by Erin Soderberg.
Description: New York: Random House, [2019] | Series: Daring Dreamers Club; 2
Summary: Part-chef, part-scientist, Piper dreams of competing on her favorite cooking
show and with the help of the rest of the Daring Dreamers Club, Milla, Zahra,
Mariana, and Ruby, she is prepared to win.
Identifiers: LCCN 2018014757 | ISBN 978-0-7364-3944-2 (hardcover) |
ISBN 978-0-7364-8265-3 (lib. bdg.) | ISBN 978-0-7364-3945-9 (ebook)
Subjects: | CYAC: Cooking—Fiction. | Friendship—Fiction. | Clubs—Fiction. |
Reality television programs—Fiction.
Classification: LCC PZ7.S685257 Pip 2019 | DDC [Fic]—dc23

Printed in the United States of America
10 9 8 7 6 5 4 3 2 1

For my editor, Rachel Poloski—
your cheerful and encouraging
personality make it so much fun
to write stories for you!
—E.S.

FiVe REAL GiRLS DaRiNG tO DREaM
LiKE THE *Princesses* THEY *love*!

Milla

Belle

Mariana

Ariel

Piper

flour Tiana

Ruby

Mulan

Zahra

Cinderella

1
COOKING UP CHAOS

Piper Andelman's experiment was going exactly as planned . . . until the smoke alarm went off.

Beeeeeeep!

Beeeeeeep!

Beeeeeeep!

Piper pressed oven mitts over her ears, trying to block out the awful sound. "Nothing to worry about!" she hollered, even though her family probably couldn't hear her over the loud beeping. "Just a little smoke, but I'll have it cleared out in a sec."

Moving quickly, Piper slid a charred, smoking

beaker away from the heat. She was turning off her hot plate when her dad, Jeremy, raced into the kitchen. He glanced around, grabbed a rolled-up newspaper off the counter, and fanned it under the wailing smoke detector. Piper flung open a window and waited for the smoke to clear.

In the midst of all the excitement, Piper's little sister, Finley, bounced around the kitchen, trying to capture everything on video with their dad's phone.

Piper's dad dropped the newspaper as soon as the smoke alarm stopped screaming. The silence was a welcome relief. "Things going well in here?" he asked in an even voice.

"All good," Piper said. She stood in front of her makeshift lab, holding her arms out wide to try to hide the chaos on the counter. Science was messy, but sometimes it was hard for parents to understand that. Especially when science took over the kitchen right before dinnertime.

Piper's dad peered around her, raising his

eyebrows when he spotted the scorched beaker and a countertop covered in sticky blue blobs. Nestled among the blobs was a mixing bowl filled with rising bread dough. A roasting pan full of chopped carrots, potatoes, and fresh herbs was prepared to go into the oven.

"It's all good. Really," Piper repeated with a smile. She sighed and added, "Dinner will be ready as soon as Mom gets home from work. I just got bored while I was waiting for the bread dough to rise, so I decided to play around a little bit. I'm testing how temperature and cooking time impact the texture of hard candy."

"Uh-huh," her dad said, folding his arms over his chest. "And what did you discover?"

Piper glanced at the still-smoldering beaker and shrugged.

"I formed my hypothesis and have started conducting tests to see if I'm right. But I can't share the results, since I haven't finished my experiment. A true scientist doesn't trust a hunch, Dad. You know I've gotta prove it first."

Finley climbed onto the counter, balancing on all fours like a cat. She plucked one of the blue blobs and popped it into her mouth. The feisty six-year-old smacked her lips together as she sucked on the slightly chewy candy.

"Meow is helping," Finley told their dad. "Meow is the taste tester and the camera lady! Meow!" Finley was going through an animal phase. For the past week, she had been starting and finishing most of her sentences with a loud meow. Piper had decided this was an improvement over her sheep phase, when she would only say *"Baaaa."*

"I see," their dad said, a smile pulling at the corners of his mouth. With a nod at the counter, he said, "Thanks for cooking tonight." He raked a hand through his short brown hair. His checkered shirt was misbuttoned, and his glasses were smudged with fingerprints.

Piper glanced at her own messy outfit through equally smudged glasses. There were sugary stains all over her apron, and she could feel her floppy knit panda hat sliding off one side of her head. It was no wonder people said she reminded them of her dad.

"Have you both finished your homework?" Dad asked.

Piper took a deep breath but didn't answer. In Finley's kindergarten world, homework was a daily coloring sheet or alphabet worksheet. Fun and games, mostly. In fifth grade, homework was the pits.

When Piper wasn't using math for science experiments or measuring recipes, she found it a total chore—and a bore. Worksheets took the *fun* out of math, and the word problems they had been working on for the past month were all so ridiculous. The questions never related to real-world problems, and the answers never made sense if you really thought about them. Piper had tried to point this out, but her teacher, Mr. Mohan, didn't seem to want to hear it. The worst part was, it was extra hard for Piper to follow the math when there was so much reading involved.

Reading and writing had *always* been a challenge for Piper, because of her dyslexia. Math seemed to take her a little longer than most people, as a result of how her mind worked. Even still, she'd never had too much trouble keeping up in math class before. But because of all the word problems they had been doing lately, Piper had started to seriously fall behind in math. And it seemed that the further behind she fell, the harder her assignments and quizzes had gotten. Since her homework was never easy *or* fun, she could come up with a million other things she would rather be doing.

"I'll do my homework after dinner," Piper promised. "You know I need a brain break after school."

"Okay," her dad said, nodding. "I'll be in my office if you need me. This deadline is killing me." He strolled out of the kitchen, trusting that Piper would clean up after herself. She always did. Well, *usually*. Or maybe it was more like *sometimes*. But she'd noticed that her dad seemed extra stressed out about work recently, so she would definitely clean up today. She wanted to stay on his good side.

Piper's dad worked from home as a graphic designer, so his "office" was just a desk in the corner of the living room. Whenever he was working on a big project, Piper offered to make the family dinner. She loved to cook, so this was one of her favorite ways to help out. Piper wasn't the smartest or most athletic Andelman (that title went to her older brother, Dan), nor was she the cutest or funniest (Finley), so Piper worked hard to try to impress her parents in other ways.

Even though making family dinners was never as exciting as any of her other food-science experiments, Piper knew that every chance she got to fool around in the kitchen was an opportunity to learn something new. She considered herself part scientist, part chef. To Piper, the words "kitchen" and "lab" meant the same thing. After all, cooking was its own kind of science.

When Piper was baking or boiling something, she knew it was important to use the right ingredients, the correct amounts, the right temperatures, and the proper amount of time— just like any other kind of science experiment. If she got the mix wrong, dinner would be a bust . . . or blow up. (Dinner had only blown up once, and it was a very messy lesson learned!)

As soon as their dad had returned to the living room, Piper grabbed the phone out of her sister's sticky hands. "Let's see what you got," she said, hitting play on the video. Both girls giggled as they watched the footage of Piper's candy experiment. The smoke alarm was a nice touch. It gave the video some extra character.

Piper wasn't at all bothered by the fact that her experiment had gone up in smoke. In fact, she was pleased. Mistakes—in both science *and* cooking—taught you something, and often led to unexpected discoveries. Food science was all about testing things and adjusting to find the right mix for your experiment. You could get different results every time and it was no big deal . . . unlike math, where making mistakes just led to a wrong answer.

"Do you think you have enough for your audition video meow?" Finley asked, popping a slice of carrot into her mouth. She made a face as she pulled a sprig of rosemary out of her mouth. "Icky prickly herbs," she said, spitting the carrot into the sink.

"Yeah," Piper said, nodding. "I should have more than enough. Thanks for helping, Fin."

She washed her hands and pushed the rest of her equipment to the side while she finished preparing dinner. As she formed balls of dough into dinner rolls, she thought about how she would put her video together.

For the past few weeks, Piper had been working on an audition video for her favorite television cooking competition, *The Future of Food*. The TV show was touring around the country, searching for the most inventive kid cooks in America. Piper was thrilled when she found out they would be filming an upcoming episode in a nearby town. She had always wanted a chance to try out for the show!

The Future of Food was different from most cooking shows, because kids were expected to use creativity and innovation in the kitchen, instead of just cooking big, fancy meals in a traditional way. Each week, the show had a different theme. Sometimes, contestants were asked to cook or bake using unusual cutting-edge gadgets. Other times, the host of the show introduced a crazy, out-there theme. Once, *The Future of Food* contestants had to cook without using any electronic tools at all. Another time, contestants were told that they lived in a future that only had potatoes and cows—so they could *only* use potato, dairy, and beef products in their dishes. One of Piper's favorite episodes required contestants to cook in a space suit, using only freeze-dried astronaut food.

Each week, three lucky and talented kid cooks were invited to compete in *The Future of Food*'s kitchen. The winner earned a $10,000 cash prize!

Being on a show like *The Future of Food* was one of Piper's big dreams, and she had every intention of making it come true. But even more importantly, she intended to win. Then she could finally prove to her family that *she* was the best at something, too.

2
DARING DREAMERS

"They picked me!" Piper blurted out, unable to keep her secret a moment longer. She had been waiting all day to share her huge news with the other four members of the Daring Dreamers Club. Now that their Tuesday advisory group meeting was officially in session, Piper bounced around Ms. Bancroft's classroom waving a piece of paper in the air. "I'm in! I'm going to be on *The Future of Food*!"

She held the sheet of paper in front of her nose and announced, "We got an email this morning that says, 'Congratulations, Piper Andelman!'

That's me! 'Based on the quality and creativity of your audition video, we would like to invite you to participate in an upcoming episode of *The Future of Food*!' " Piper twisted a lock of her hair and looked around. "Then it goes on and on with a whole bunch of details about dates and times, where I go for filming, and stuff like that. Can you believe it?"

"This is so exciting!" Milla Bannister-Cook said, squeezing her best friend tight. Sweet, adventure-loving Milla had been friends with Piper for years, so she knew just how much an opportunity like this meant to her. "When do they film the episode?"

"In less than three weeks," Piper told her friends and Ms. Bancroft. "I have a zillion things to do to get ready. I'm going to be cooking so much the next few weeks!"

"We'll help you!" Ruby Fawcett said, speaking on behalf of everyone. Ruby was the smallest member of the Daring Dreamers Club, but she had the biggest voice. In fact, Ruby and her twin brother, Henry, were two of the most outspoken—and sporty—members of the fifth-grade class at Walter Roy Elementary. Loyal, clever, tell-it-like-it-is Ruby was the kind of person everyone wanted on their team. "What can we do to make sure you're ready to win?"

"I can be a taste tester or a sous-chef, if you want," Mariana Sanchez offered with a shy smile. Though Mari was quiet, she was also one of the most fearless people Piper had ever met. She loved trying new things, and she was good at almost everything she tried. "I'm not a picky eater, and I'm pretty good at chopping. My abuela loves to cook, and she's taught me stuff. She makes the most amazing chicken mole you've ever eaten."

"You know Chip will happily eat any scraps that aren't fit for human consumption," Milla said, laughing. Chocolate Chip was Milla's pet pig, and he loved snacking on Piper's creations—even the yucky, failed experiments.

"I probably won't be much help with tasting, but I'd be happy to help with cleanup duties." Milla was allergic to nuts and dairy, so she had to be careful about what she ate.

"Can I help you figure out your outfit for the show?" Zahra Sharif asked. Hardworking, independent Zahra loved designing clothes, as well as making mosaics and painting, in her free time. She was the most artistic member of the Daring Dreamers Club. "We have to find something for you to wear that's going to really pop on TV. And I would *love* to help you come up with some fun ideas for plating your food. Your dishes need to look creative and appealing if you want to win, right?"

The offers of help were shouted out, voices layering on top of voices, as everyone grew more and more excited about Piper's television debut. The Daring Dreamers Club had only been around since the first week of fifth grade, when the five girls were assigned to the same fifth-grade

advisory group at school. But in that short time, Piper, Milla, Ruby, Zahra, and Mariana had already grown very close.

Their school's principal had started the advisory groups to help fifth graders prepare for the independence of middle school. Every fifth grader was put in a small group made up of peers and a teacher-advisor. During their twice-weekly meetings, these groups talked about issues and challenges, goals and dreams.

Piper's group had been lucky enough to get Ms. Bancroft, the school's new music teacher, as their advisor. Ms. B was one of the most unique and inspiring women any of them had ever met. She loved encouraging her group to dream big and reach for the stars—which is why the girls had named themselves the Daring Dreamers Club.

Piper couldn't quite believe one of her big dreams was already coming true—and to make the dream even sweeter, she was going to *win*!

"Guess what?" she said, smiling wider. "I get enough visitor passes that all of you will be able to come watch the show being filmed!" Everyone cheered.

Ms. Bancroft spoke for the first time that meeting. "I think I must be a little out of the loop . . . ," she said. "What exactly is *The Future of Food*? Some sort of television show, I'm assuming?"

Ruby's mouth gaped open. "You haven't seen it, Ms. B?"

Ms. Bancroft shrugged. "I'm more of a movie buff. And frankly, cooking isn't my strong suit. I'm a canned-soup-and-takeout kind of chef."

Piper groaned. "Whoa, whoa, whoa . . . You can't *cook*?"

"I didn't say I *can't*," Ms. Bancroft said, laughing. "I just prefer not to. My kitchen experiments never end well."

"Okay, this could be a problem," Piper said. One of the things that made *The Future of*

Food fun was that the host—who called herself the Kitchen Wizard—loved surprise challenges. Contestants never got to just *cook*. There was always some sort of twist.

Piper had watched every episode of *The Future of Food* and knew that the Kitchen Wizard sometimes even made contestants work with a friend or family member to create their dish. Piper wanted to be prepared for *anything* the show's host might throw at her, so she had to make sure her audience members were ready, too! What if they were called up to cook with her?

"If you're going to be in the audience as my guest," Piper said firmly, "you're going to need to practice a few cooking basics first. You all probably should. They could call any one of you onto the set, and I need to be sure you know what you're doing in a kitchen before I can risk having you there with me. They've called on audience members during three out of thirty-seven shows, which means there's an eight percent chance they'll make me work with one of you during one of my surprise challenges. . . ."

"Does this mean we all get to go to Piper's Cooking School?" Ruby said, laughing.

"I have a better idea," Piper said, thinking quickly. "What's everyone doing after school on Thursday?"

"I have soccer practice at six-thirty," Ruby said. "But I'm free until then."

"Same," Mari echoed. "Swimming at six. But I could maybe skip it. Why?"

Piper explained, "My family volunteers at a place called Helping Hands on the last Thursday of every month. We make meals for people who can't cook for themselves because they are seriously ill or disabled. Do you guys want to come along? It would be a good place to practice some basics; Helping Hands is where I learned a lot of fundamentals. My brother was a lousy cook until we started volunteering, and now he's not totally useless in the kitchen."

Everyone agreed that it was a great idea, so they made a plan to join Piper's family during their shift at Helping Hands on Thursday. "What about you, Ms. B?" Piper asked. "You wanna come, too?"

"It sounds like a really nice idea," their advisor said hesitantly.

"Come on, Ms. Bancroft," Milla urged. "It'll be fun."

"Please?" Piper begged. "You've got to start somewhere."

"Okay, I'm in," Ms. Bancroft said with a smile. "I guess I can't live on takeout and frozen dinners forever, much as I'd like to dream it's possible." She laughed the deep, rumbling laugh that Piper loved and said, "Now that we have that settled, we really need to spend the last few minutes of today's session discussing your next journal writing assignment."

Piper groaned inwardly. She *loved* meetings of the Daring Dreamers Club, but she did *not* love the journal writing assignments. Unlike Milla, who would spend her day writing if she could, Piper found writing overwhelming and frustrating. It took her a really long time to write a whole page in her journal, and that was time she would much rather spend testing experiments and new recipes. "Aw, Ms. B," she muttered. "Maybe we could just skip the journal assignment this week? I'll bake you a batch of homemade cookies if you say yes!"

"I'm afraid we can't do that," Ms. Bancroft said kindly. "Journal writing is a required part of advisory. However, I would like to get your input on the next assignment, to make sure we're all on the same page." She gestured for the girls to take a seat and then went on. "Remind me what you all thought of the princess project?"

"I loved the princess assignment, Ms. B," Ruby blurted out. She glanced around at the rest of the group and shrugged. "I know I was a little *meh* about your journal assignment at first, but I actually had fun finding connections between myself and Mulan. She's fierce and clever. Like me!"

For the group's first journal writing assignment, Ms. Bancroft had asked each girl in the club to think about a Disney Princess they connected with or felt inspired by, and explain why. With one quick look around the music classroom, anyone could see that Ms. Bancroft was seriously into princesses. The walls were plastered with pictures of Belle and Cinderella and Snow White and Ariel . . . along with inspiring quotes from dozens of important people.

During their first meeting, Ms. B had told the group that watching Disney movies had helped her dare to dream big as a kid, which is what inspired her to pick princesses as their first advisory journal theme.

"I liked it, too," Milla chimed in. "And I definitely felt more comfortable writing about my dreams of adventure when I was also writing about Belle and *Beauty and the Beast*."

"I thought it was fun to think about how much I have in common with Ariel," Mari added. "I rewatched *The Little Mermaid* with my sisters this weekend, and I haven't been able to stop singing 'Part of Your World' since!"

"What about you, Zahra and Piper?" Ms. Bancroft prompted.

"I enjoyed the assignment," Zahra said thoughtfully. "I'd actually really like to continue with the princess theme, if we can. I feel like I've just started to figure out how I relate to Cinderella, and I think it would be interesting to keep writing about my connection to her in my journal."

"Me too," Piper said, nodding. She had always found an easy parallel between herself and Tiana from *The Princess and the Frog*. Surely she would be able to find more things she could write about in her journal if she had her favorite princess as a partner. "Do you think," Piper began, "that we could keep writing about our princesses all year?

I mean, what if we used the *same* princess for inspiration every week? It could be a sort of theme for our journals."

There was a murmur of agreement from the other girls. Ms. Bancroft looked around the circle, her smile widening. "Of course," she said. "There are some great things to explore in the worlds and minds of our princesses, and having a partner on this journey through fifth grade will hopefully help each of you develop new insight into yourselves."

When Ms. Bancroft said this, Piper and Ruby exchanged small smiles—they both loved Ms. B to pieces, but the way she worded things sometimes made them giggle.

Ms. Bancroft cleared her throat and went on, "If we all agree, then I have your next assignment, Daring Dreamers: At some point, every princess must face a fear or overcome an obstacle standing in her way. Using your princess for inspiration, talk about a time you've had to confront a fear or deal with a difficult issue. Sound good?"

Everyone nodded. While Piper shoved her journal into her backpack, she turned to Milla and whispered, "Compared to Tiana's, my life looks pretty easy. At least I've never been turned into a frog!"

Piper

Assignment: Using your princess for inspiration, talk about a time you've had to face a fear or overcome an obstacle standing in your way.

I guess I should thank my lucky stars that I've never been turned into a frog. At least that's one thing I've got going for me. But I have a feeling I'm supposed to dig a little deeper (Ha ha! Get it? That's a song from <u>The Princess and the Frog</u>!) with this assignment, huh?

Maybe you've read my school file and already know this, but I found out in second grade that I have dyslexia. I guess that's sort of an obstacle that stands in my way. I sometimes mix up my letters, and I'm a slow reader and writer (I should get bonus points, since getting these journals right takes me forever, Ms. B!).

It took me a really long time to learn to

read, and for a while I worried that maybe it was because I'm not very smart. I thought my brother had gotten all the brains in the family and there weren't any left for me. But then I learned more about _why_ I have so much trouble reading and writing, and now I know it's not my fault.

Did you know there are some supersmart and creative people who had dyslexia? Like the artist Pablo Picasso, Apple founder Steve Jobs, movie director Steven Spielberg . . . And no one's one hundred percent sure, but there are lots of articles that say Agatha Christie did, too (it's crazy to think that an author could be dyslexic since her whole job was working with words!). They are all really important creators, so I'm in some pretty good company.

Dyslexia is the reason I started playing around with my own inventions in the kitchen. I've always liked to cook, but it was hard for me to follow written recipes. So I

started making up my own. I like figuring things out for myself, and when I'm in the kitchen, I get to do just that! That's one way I've worked around my challenge.

I try not to let my reading and writing troubles get me down. But I hate that I have such a hard time in school. My brother, Dan, is a total smarty-pants, and it seems like everything comes easily to him. And Finley, my little sister, is already reading, and she just started kindergarten. I hate messing up in school, and I really don't like having to ask for extra help. And knowing my brother and sister are super perfect makes things even worse.

At my house, it sometimes feels a little bit like I'm competing with my siblings. Every time I bring home a report card or test, I know my parents are going to be disappointed it's nothing like my brother's. And my sister is always saying and doing funny (or naughty) stuff that gets everyone's attention and makes people laugh. It sometimes feels like it's me against them. Whoever stands out more wins. So that's why I need to win <u>The Future of Food</u>. Then everyone will see that I'm the best at something, too!

Whoa. I wrote <u>way</u> more than a page this time. Go, me! (Does this mean I can skip next week's assignment?)

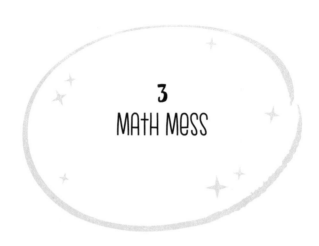

3
MATH MESS

Piper dropped her head into her hands and groaned. She had been staring at her math workbook for over an hour (maybe more like fifteen minutes, but it *felt* like an hour), but nothing was clicking. The longer she stared at the page, the more the word problems swirled into a mixed-up stew of letters and numbers that made absolutely no sense to her.

"Want some help?" Dan asked through a mouthful of freshly baked cheddar crackers. Piper was pleased to see that her brother was enjoying her latest creation. She had spent the afternoon *trying* to make bread. To keep things interesting, she'd decided to play around with moisture levels and rise time. The fact that the dough had turned into crackers was a mistake, but it was one of those experiments that fell into the category of "happy accident." Instead of the flaky cheddar loaf she had set out to make, she'd ended up with tasty, crisp crackers instead. They tasted a little bit like the matzo her family ate during Passover—but with added flavor baked in!

Dan leaned over Piper's shoulder and ran his finger across the page. "First you need to figure out how many muffins Mr. Mancini brought to the bake sale, and then you'll—"

"I know," Piper snapped, brushing cracker crumbs off her math workbook. "I can figure it out myself."

Dan lifted his eyebrows. "*Oookay,* I was offering to help."

Piper felt bad for snapping at him, but it was sometimes annoying having a brother who was a total know-it-all. Everything came really easily to Dan. And Piper had never liked taking help from anyone. Back in kindergarten and first grade, she had often been pulled out of class for extra sight-word practice in the hall. She'd hated the way she felt singled out when someone called her name and removed her from the larger class activities. It almost felt like she was wearing a sign that read BAD STUDENT.

One of the reasons Piper had always loved playing around in the kitchen was that she was the only one in her family who loved cooking, so it was the one place where no one could say she was doing things wrong. Plus, creating her own recipes and experiments meant there was no right or wrong outcome. In food science, what-ever happened happened. She got to be the boss, and Piper alone knew when she'd succeeded or failed. Of course, she always jotted her results down in her lab notebook, no matter how things turned out. It was important to keep a record of

her experiments. Mistakes helped her learn and become a better cook!

Piper draped her arm across her math workbook and pretended to scribble something on the page. While she drew curlicues, she thought about the quiz she had crammed into the back of her notebook. She had done terribly. Her score was *so* low that she had to have one of her parents sign it to prove she'd shown it to them.

She really didn't want her parents to see the quiz, but Mr. Mohan was the kind of teacher who would call them if she didn't bring it back with a signature. Piper was nervous to show her mom and dad. What if they got mad at her? Still, she knew that she just needed to work harder and she would eventually catch up. That was her hope, at least.

As Piper doodled cupcakes on the edge of her paper, her mom strolled into the dining room. She hollered, "What is one of your biggest weaknesses?"

"Huh?" Piper asked, looking up. Her mom, Renee, grinned at her as she gestured toward the living room.

A second later, Piper's dad called, "Am I allowed to say 'my biceps'?"

Piper's mom laughed. "I don't think any companies will care about your arm muscles. I meant, what's one of your greatest weaknesses in a *business* sense."

"What are you guys talking about?" Piper asked.

Her dad wandered into the dining room and snagged a cracker off the table. He glanced at his wife, then explained, "Well . . . I have an interview on Thursday. Your mom is helping me dust off the ol' résumé and practice my interviewing skills."

"An interview for what?" Dan asked, pouring himself a glass of milk. He downed it, then refilled the glass. Piper was grateful he wasn't drinking straight out of the carton.

"A full-time gig," their dad said casually. "I'm sure nothing will come of it, but I figure it can't hurt to give it a shot."

Piper gaped at him. "What kind of full-time gig?" she asked.

"A full-time design job," he explained.

"Like, in an office?" she asked.

Her dad laughed. "Yeah, in an office."

"When did you decide to get a full-time job?" Dan asked. Piper was relieved to discover she wasn't the only one surprised by this news.

For as long as Piper could remember, her dad had worked from home doing part-time free-lance graphic design projects. Her mom had a regular office job, something to do with marketing or advertising. But her dad had always been around in the morning to get them out the door to school and welcome them home at the end of the day. In a slightly panicked voice, Piper asked, "How's that going to work?"

"First of all," their mom said, settling in at the

table across from her, "nothing's been decided yet. This is just one interview, and it's a cool opportunity."

"Now that Finley is in kindergarten," her dad added, "I have a lot more time on my hands. A full-time job would really help with the family finances, so I've been looking around a bit. I'm not sure *this* is the right job, but it's worth exploring. We haven't talked to you guys about it because I have no idea what will come of it."

Piper swallowed, her tongue feeling thick in her mouth. She couldn't believe her dad hadn't said something about this interview. She liked having him around before and after school, and she didn't want that to change. Besides, she reasoned, if her dad had to go to an office every day, she and Finley might be stuck taking orders from *Dan*. Finley had already gone to bed for the night, but Piper could predict that her little sister would freak out if she heard this news.

"Are we broke?" Piper asked.

Piper's dad snorted out a laugh. She didn't understand what was so funny about her question. "No, we're not broke," he said. He set his glasses on the table and then rubbed the bridge of his nose. "Work has been a little hot-and-cold lately, but it's nothing for you guys to worry about. I'm just exploring options right now, okay?"

"Okay," Piper muttered.

"How's your homework going?" her mom asked suddenly, nudging Piper's notebook.

"Great," Piper lied, draping her arm across the open page again. Dan gave her a look that told her he knew she wasn't being entirely honest. But Piper wasn't about to admit she was having problems. If her parents were stressed about her dad's interview and money, the last thing they needed to worry about was her fifth-grade math homework.

"I'm happy to see you working on math," her mom said. "I've noticed you've been spending a lot of time in the kitchen this week. We still have our deal, right?"

Piper cringed. Her mom had made her promise that her preparations for *The Future of Food* wouldn't get in the way of her schoolwork. "Totally," she lied again. "I'm actually working ahead so I can spend the weekend in my lab, or as you call it, the kitchen."

"Good plan." Her mom smiled and nodded, trusting her completely.

Piper immediately felt guilty for lying. While her mom continued to quiz her dad with more practice interview questions, Piper stared down at her unfinished homework. Once again, her mind wandered to the paper crammed into the back of her notebook. Now definitely wasn't the best time to show her parents the failed quiz—she would wait until after her dad's interview, and after *The Future of Food*. By then, she would have caught up with the rest of the class, and her parents would see that one bad score was no big deal.

With time, she could figure it out on her own. She knew that was what Tiana would tell her, too. Her favorite princess had taught her that hard work was the secret to success, and it was the only way to get what you wanted. She didn't need anyone's help to get caught up. Besides, her parents had kept her dad's job search a secret. So her keeping one little quiz inside her notebook for a few extra days was no big deal, either. Piper just hoped her parents would see it that way, too.

4
HELPING HANDS

On Thursday after school, the Daring Dreamers met outside the front doors of Walter Roy Elementary. Piper's mom had left work early to pick up the girls and drive them and Finley over to Helping Hands for their volunteer shift. Ms. Bancroft was going to meet them there.

Usually, Piper's dad would be the one picking the girls up from school to go to Helping Hands, since he had the more flexible schedule. But he had to miss their family's volunteer shift that week to go to his interview. Piper couldn't help but see this as a very bad sign for how *everything* would change if he got a full-time job.

Finley sang and meowed the whole way to the Helping Hands kitchen. By the time Piper's mom pulled their minivan into the lot at the volunteer center, every single one of them had memorized the lyrics to "How Far I'll Go" from *Moana.* Piper loved *Moana,* but sometimes she wished Finley would change favorite movies as often as she changed favorite animals. They had been listening to the same soundtrack for six months. It would be nice to hear a few different songs from time to time.

Inside the Helping Hands building, Piper pointed out lockers where they could stash their stuff. When Ms. Bancroft arrived, the girls were pulling on hairnets and washing their hands with strong-smelling soap.

"It's nice of you to join us," Piper's mom said to Ms. Bancroft, holding out her hand. "I'm Renee—Piper's mom."

"I'm Amy," Ms. Bancroft said. "I've been

looking for a way to connect with the community since I moved to town this summer, so it's wonderful of Piper to include me."

While the two adults got acquainted, Piper led her friends on a tour of the small, crowded space. There were two business offices at the back of the building—"This is where the full-time staff works," she explained—but most of the area was filled with industrial-sized refrigerators, giant ovens and stoves, and stainless steel counters for food prep.

"I started coming here with my parents when I was about Finley's age," Piper told the others. "When you're little, you don't get to use knives or be near the stoves. But they still let you help out by decorating food delivery bags or making cards for the people receiving meals."

As soon as Ms. Bancroft joined them, Piper led them through the kitchen, pointing out dry goods, knives, and cutting boards. "One of the things I love about working at Helping Hands is that, as soon as you turn eight, you get to be involved in the actual cooking part of the job. They need all the help they can get to make as many meals as they do." She noticed that Ms. Bancroft had an uneasy look on her face. "Don't worry, Ms. B. There are easy jobs and less-easy jobs. Right after my eighth birthday, I learned a lot of cooking basics during my shifts here: chopping, sautéing, oven safety, food safety. It's all important stuff to master when you want to be a good cook."

"Welcome!" a voice boomed. The group spun around to see where the loud voice came from. A man the size of a small refrigerator—with tattooed arms, a shaved head, thick black eyebrows, and wearing an enormous flowered apron—filled the space behind them. "I see we have some newbies today, eh?" He held up one of his massive, pawlike hands and gave Piper a high five. Finley raced over to give the man a hug.

"Hi, Duck," Piper said. "These are my friends from school, and this is our teacher-advisor, Ms. Bancroft. They're here to help today. Guys, this is Duck. He's the boss. Whatever he says goes. Trust me, you don't want to get on his bad side."

Ruby and Mariana exchanged nervous looks.

"She's kidding, of course," Duck said with a wide smile. "Anyone who knows me knows I'm a big softie, and I don't really have a bad side. Anyone who knows *Piper* knows *she's* the boss whenever she's in the kitchen. Isn't that right?"

Everyone laughed.

Duck folded his arms across his barrel chest. "In all seriousness, I'm always grateful to have help around here, so don't worry about making mistakes while you're learning the ropes. The most important things are being safe and having fun. A few shifts in this kitchen and you'll be a cooking pro. Isn't that right, Finley?" Finley wrapped her hands around Duck's arm and started swinging from it as if he were a tree.

"Meow," she said. Finley pushed her feet against Duck's thigh and climbed, still holding on to his arm with both hands. Duck didn't seem to notice that he had a six-year-old dangling off his body.

"Has Piper told you about our program?" Duck asked, gesturing to a wall filled with first names. "These are the names of some of the people we're serving right now, as well as people we've served in the past," he explained. "Our team of volunteers helps people with cancer, HIV, AIDS, ALS, and MS, as well as a few people recovering from major surgery. Our goal at Helping Hands is to assist people who can't take care of themselves by providing them with delicious, nutritious meals. The last thing they should have to worry about is cooking." Duck patted the wall of names and said, "This wall represents my family, our community. When you help out here, they become a part of your family, too."

While Duck strolled around the kitchen,

finishing the tour, he told the group a little more about why he had started Helping Hands. "This organization began in my home kitchen several years ago. I had two friends dealing with life-threatening illnesses at the same time, and I wanted to find some way to help. I started making them meals once a week. I quickly saw that something easy for me brought my friends a lot of joy and relief, so I began cooking them meals every other day. Soon, I expanded to serve a few more people, and things grew from there. We feed anywhere from fifty to sixty-five people a week, and we're always looking for opportunities to expand our reach."

"Do you have volunteers working here every day?" Zahra asked.

"That's the goal," Duck said. "The more help we get, the more people we can serve. I can't cook enough food for everyone by myself, so we've built a solid group of volunteers. Some people come once a week, some only when they can squeeze it in—any time is better than no time at all."

"How do you pay for all the food?" Mariana asked.

"Good question," Duck replied. "We get donations from individuals, and we apply for grants. Whatever comes in as funding goes back out to the Helping Hands community in the way of nutritious, delicious meals."

"What if someone has allergies?" Milla asked.

Duck nodded. "We talk about allergies, religious beliefs, and dietary needs and preferences with all our clients before their first delivery. I make sure everyone is getting the kind of food they like and can eat. People undergoing chemotherapy for cancer have different food needs from someone who's having trouble with muscle control. We have to take a whole bunch of factors into consideration. It's a bit of a juggling act to get everyone taken care of sometimes, but it keeps things interesting. Chefs like it when things are interesting, am I right, Piper?" He winked at her.

Piper gave him a thumbs-up. No one else had questions, so Duck talked them through the process for cooking and packaging the food. "Once you've cooked today's main course— which is butternut squash, carrot, and lentil stew—it gets packed up and delivered to members of our Helping Hands family. Simple as that. It takes a village to make it all come together, but we get it done and make some lives a little easier."

Every time Piper heard Duck talk through the Helping Hands mission statement, she got goose bumps. She loved cooking and experimenting in the kitchen for fun, but nothing compared to that feeling she got when they were cleaning up the kitchen at the end of a shift. She loved helping others. She was so happy she could share this experience with her fellow Daring Dreamers.

As soon as everyone was suited up with aprons, hairnets, and rubber gloves, Duck walked them through the day's recipe. He explained things quickly, but Piper kept up with his rapid-fire instructions.

"Well, that's that. I'll leave you to get started, and I'll check back to see how things are going in a bit," Duck said with a wave. "Usually I stick around to oversee my volunteers, but I trust that Piper and Renee can answer any questions you might have. They're some of the best, and I know you're in good hands. Finley, I could use your help in the office making some birthday cards for a few of our folks." And then they were gone.

"He left," Ruby said, staring after Duck. "What are we supposed to do now?"

"Now we cook," Piper said. She giggled when she saw how overwhelmed her friends looked. And Ms. B looked *terrified* as she rolled a giant butternut squash back and forth on the counter. "Trust me," she added. "You'll relax when you start working. It seems like a lot at first, but we just have to break it down into little steps and it will all work out."

"But . . . ," Milla said, looking at the mounds of vegetables and lentils and cans of stock on the gleaming stainless steel counters. "He expects us to turn all *this* into *stew?*"

"That's how you cook," Piper said simply. "It's kitchen science magic. We'll start from the beginning, and you'll see how simple it is."

For the next hour, Piper and her mom showed the group how to chop vegetables, sauté onions, prepare lentils, and knead dough for the rustic French loaves they were making to accompany the soup.

Mariana's tough swimmer's muscles made her an expert dough kneader, so she took the lead on baking the bread. Zahra discovered she could dice onions like a pro, and they didn't even make her cry! So Piper left both of her friends at their stations and told them to holler if they needed any help.

Meanwhile, Milla, Ruby, and Ms. Bancroft took on carrot-chopping duties. But none of them could get the hang of it. After fifteen minutes, the three of them had only managed to peel and chop four carrots (while Piper and her mom had peeled and cubed *all* the butternut squash). The carrot team was so busy laughing and teasing one another about their sad kitchen skills, Piper began to wonder if they were even trying. Frustrated and impatient, she suggested she take over.

"Fine by me," Ruby said, shoving her peeler and cutting board toward Piper. She wiped her hands on her apron, plucked a ball of bread dough off Mariana's workstation, and tossed it high into the air.

"But if you do it for us," Milla pointed out, "we won't learn or get better."

Piper considered this and realized Milla was right. One of the reasons she had taken the group to Helping Hands was so they could practice their skills and learn. Much as she didn't like getting help herself, she knew she had to figure out how to support them rather than just taking over. In both science and cooking, she knew, it was best to take things step by step. Patiently, Piper demonstrated curling the fingers and thumb of her non-knife hand into a claw grip (to protect her fingers and allow her to dice the carrots a little faster). Then she gave them a few tips that had made her feel more comfortable with a knife and hard veggies when she had first starting chopping. In no time, the carrot team had doubled their output. By then, Mariana had finished the bread and come over to help with the veggies.

Piper's mom settled in at the stove, and soon the kitchen smelled amazing. Once all the veggies had been dumped into the stew and it was bubbling in a giant pot, Piper ladled out little samples for everyone to try. "You always have to try your food before serving it to others," she told them.

"A little more salt?" Mariana asked, tilting her head to one side.

"Definitely," Piper agreed, then sprinkled a bit into the pot.

"It's really delicious," Zahra said, her eyes wide. "And the colors blend together beautifully."

"We made this," Ruby said. "Ms. B, we *made* this!" She and Ms. Bancroft exchanged high fives.

Everyone pitched in to help with cleanup. They wiped down counters with sanitizer, swept the floors, and put all their waste in the designated bins. The kitchen was gleaming in no time.

By the time Duck and Finley returned, the three-hour shift was almost over and the group had fifty portions of stew packaged up and ready to go. The individual-sized bread loaves were cooling invitingly on one of the long counters.

Piper beamed at her friends. She waved her hands in front of the end result and said, "And that, my friends, is how it's done. Kitchen science magic!"

Zahra

I've been thinking about this journal question a lot these past few days. Cinderella had to overcome many obstacles in her life (not fitting in with her family, the loss of her father, two bullying step sisters), but one of the things I most admire about her is that she always kept a positive attitude, even when the people closest to her treated her unkindly. She constantly tried to bring joy to others' lives, despite the fact that her own life had its challenges. I'm sure she felt afraid many times, but she somehow kept a good outlook.

You've probably already noticed this, but there are only twelve girls at our elementary school who wear the hijab. I'm proud to be a Muslim, but there are times when people around town look at me in a certain way when they see my headscarf. Most of the time, it's not an unfriendly look (I can tell a lot of people are just curious). So I always respond with a smile, and people will often smile back. But sometimes, the way people stare or react to my hijab makes me feel uncomfortable. (Milla talked about feeling this way, too, because of her scar. I totally get it.)

Once, a car full of teenage boys stopped near our house. The boys rolled down their windows and shouted a lot of really rude words at my brother and me while we were playing outside. I felt very afraid. I try not to be afraid, but when stuff like that happens, it's hard to shake off the fear. I wish I could help these boys understand that wearing my scarf is a way to honor my faith, and it's an important part of who I am. No matter how people treat me, I try to respond with kindness, compassion, and understanding, because that's also an important part of who I am.

Another thing I love about Cinderella is that she always went out of her way to be extra kind to animals and to help others (no matter how big, small, or important they were). I always try to act that way, too. Service and giving are both very important in my family. (Did you know that one of the key pillars of the Islamic faith is charity?) I volunteer at my dad's childcare center every Wednesday after school, as an act of service. And every year, my brother, parents, and I each choose a charity we are going to donate our money to. I save a portion of my allowance each week, and my parents match the amount I have saved up at the end of the year.

I loved volunteering at Helping Hands with Piper and the rest of the Daring Dreamers Club this week. It was fun to be a part of another family's service traditions. Maybe I should take everyone to my dad's childcare center sometime!

5
SURPRISE CHALLENGES

After their visit to Helping Hands, the Daring Dreamers made plans to meet at Piper's house on Saturday to help her prepare for *The Future of Food*. Milla had gone home with Piper a few times after school to keep Piper company while she tested out some new recipes, but the other girls were eager to help her get ready for the competition, too. Throughout the week, the club had been brainstorming ideas for how they could help her practice before the show. And now it was finally time to put a few of those ideas into action!

When the doorbell rang on Saturday afternoon, Finley bounded to the front door on all fours and greeted Zahra with a loud "Meow!"

"Hello, Finley," Zahra said, patting her on the head. "I brought you something." Zahra held out a pair of fluffy pink-and-black-striped cat ears mounted on a plush headband.

Finley settled the ears on top of her head and pawed at Zahra's leg. "Meow *love* them," she said. "Thank you!" She purred as she climbed on all fours up the stairs to her bedroom. Finley had promised to stay out of the way while Piper and her friends were working in the kitchen. But Piper doubted she would keep her promise for long. Luckily, Finley had brought her class's pet frog home to take care of over the weekend, so that would keep her occupied for a while. And Piper had bribed her sister to stay out of their way by making animal-shaped fruit jellies with her that morning. (It had been fun using pectin to play around with shapes and texture!) But even with a belly full of lime-flavored jellies, Piper knew Finley would sneak down to be a part of the kitchen action eventually. Her sister didn't like missing out on any kind of fun.

"Did you make those ears?" Piper asked. Zahra nodded; she loved sewing and making things. "That was super nice of you. But you know Fin's probably going to pick a new animal she wants to be next week."

Zahra laughed. "That's okay. I'll give her fresh ears when her cat phase is over. I make stuff like this for the dress-up bin at my dad's childcare center all the time."

"Your dad works in a childcare center?" Piper asked. "Like, a day care?"

"Yeah," Zahra said. "He owns it. He's also the childcare center's lead preschool teacher. He loves working with kids."

"Seriously? I had no idea," Piper said.

"How would you? It never came up," Zahra said, shrugging.

The next few minutes were a whirlwind of activity as all the other girls showed up. As soon as everyone had arrived, Piper led her friends to the kitchen.

"See what you think of this," she said, pushing a plate of dried fruit across the counter to her friends. "My mom borrowed a food dehydrator from one of her coworkers so I could practice using it before the show," she explained. "There are always tons of weird gadgets and tools on set that contestants are supposed to use, so I want to be sure I'm familiar with as many of them as possible before filming day!"

Ruby popped a wrinkled mango slice into her mouth. "Yummy." She grabbed a slice of strawberry, then another and another.

Milla plucked a light-as-air piece of banana off the plate and nibbled on one corner. "Whoa, this banana is crispy. That's kind of weird. You don't expect a banana to crunch."

"Try this next," Piper instructed, shaking

something brown and crumbly out of a bowl and into Mariana's palm.

"What is it?" Mari asked, scrunching her nose. "No offense, but it looks like rotten meat."

"Just try it," Piper said with a laugh. "Then guess."

Mariana took a small taste and her eyes went wide. "It tastes like ice cream. But it's not wet—or cold."

"Ding ding ding!" Piper cried out. "It *is* ice cream. Well, sort of. I've been trying to figure out how to freeze-dry different things. You know, like astronaut food? The consistency is all wrong since I don't have an actual freeze dryer. But I've been experimenting with some other ways of getting the moisture out of food, and I'm finally coming close."

"You are *so* talented," Milla said. "I don't know how you come up with all your ideas for what to do in the kitchen."

Piper shrugged. "Food science is really just

a bunch of what-ifs. I taste or cook something, and then I think *what if?* Like, *what if* ice cream didn't have to be cold? Or *what if* super-ripe fruit didn't drip down your chin? Or *what if* I cooked something with more heat or less yeast or added a flavor or whatever? It's fun to play around with ordinary stuff and see what happens."

She pushed the empty plate aside. "I still want to try using a smoker and an immersion circulator sometime. And, of course, I'd like to do more with infusion. . . ." Piper trailed off, noticing the other girls' blank looks. Laughing, she explained, "Those are a few of the tools contestants have used on past episodes. A smoker gives your creations a sort of woodsy flavor. I've never been a big fan of smoked flavors myself, but I guess it could be useful in the right situation, with the right combinations of stuff." With an excited look in her eye, she went on, "And an immersion circulator is a tool used in sous vide cooking—"

"Sue who?" Ruby asked.

Piper laughed. "Sous vide," she said. "It's a French term. You cook food in a plastic pouch that's all sealed up. And an *infuser* . . . you guys know about infusers, right?"

Mari shook her head, eyes wide. "Uh, no."

Piper pushed her glasses up her nose and said, "Tea is made using infusion. And you know that yummy lemon- or cucumber-flavored water they sometimes have in the lobbies of hotels? Infusion is when you soak something in liquid to extract the flavor, then use that flavor in other things."

"You are going to be seriously amazing on *The Future of Food*," Ruby declared.

Piper flushed with pride. "Thanks. I hope you're right."

Ruby went on, "My brother and I watched a few more episodes of the show online last night, and Henry is one hundred percent sure you're going to win. Twins don't *always* agree, but I'm totally with him on this."

"I just wish I knew who I'm going to be competing against," Piper said wistfully. "I could be up against a movie star, or some supersmart child prodigy who's been cooking since she was two, or some flashy YouTuber who has ten million followers . . . who knows!"

"I feel bad for whoever's competing against *you*," Zahra said. "They have no idea what they're going up against. You're definitely going to be a superstar."

"Thank you," Piper said, momentarily taken aback by Zahra's kind words. She wasn't used to being the star of *anything*. She could already imagine what it would feel like to hold that $10,000 check and stand under the confetti and swirling lights, with the champion's golden spatula in her hand. Her parents would run onto the set and congratulate her, and—

She shook her head to clear it, trying to remember that *dreaming* about her win was only going to get her so far. She could dream big, but if she wanted that dream to come true, she had some serious work to do! Pulling an apron out of the drawer, Piper said, "Well, anyway, I don't have any control over the other kids I'll be competing against, but I *can* try to prepare myself for the surprise challenges. I'm sure there will be a few difficult obstacles I need to overcome before I can win. Are you guys ready to test me?"

Piper's friends had come up with a series of difficult challenges to help her prepare for what she might have to face during her episode. The other girls exchanged excited smiles.

"We're totally ready. The more important question is: Are you?" Ruby asked.

Piper tied her apron and tucked her tangled braids inside a fluffy blue-and-white knit hat. Then she rubbed her hands together and said, "Let's get cookin'."

6
BABY FOOD BLUES

Zahra dropped a quilted bag on Piper's kitchen counter and reached inside. With a flourish, she pulled out a small glass jar and held it up. "Your first surprise challenge," she said with a sly smile. "Baby food!" She twisted off the lid and held the jar in front of Piper's nose.

Piper sniffed it. "Interesting. Sweet potatoes?"

"Yep," Zahra said with a nod. She pulled two more jars out of her bag. "We also have peach-banana puree and mashed green peas. I got them from my dad's work." She held one of the jars like it was a microphone and then said in a funny announcer voice, "For this surprise challenge, you will need to convert this baby food into a delicious dessert—and make it look appealing, too. You have thirty minutes. Good luck!"

Milla set a timer on her watch. Then Zahra and the rest of the Daring Dreamers Club settled in on one side of the breakfast bar, watching as Piper got to work in the kitchen.

Without using any kind of recipe, she quickly whipped up a batch of pastry dough, talking through each step as she cooked. "I'm going to make tartlets," she explained. She stirred and kneaded and rolled, working in a flurry of flour, butter, and eggs. As soon as she'd finished rolling the dough and began cutting it into little circles, Ruby held up her hand.

"Stop!" she cried. "Time for another surprise challenge!"

Piper clapped. "Hit me!" she said cheerfully.

"From now on, you can *only* use your left hand for cooking," Ruby said, giggling.

"But I'm left-handed," Piper reminded her.

"Then you can only use your *right* hand for cooking," Ruby said. "Good luck!"

Piper got back to work, moving much more slowly than she had before. She kept dropping ingredients, and little splats of baby food littered the countertop.

Finley slipped into the kitchen, meowing around the mess. She was pulling a jump rope that she had attached to a skateboard. Riding atop the skateboard was the kindergarten's class frog, staring out at the world from inside his plastic cage. "Can meow help you?" Finley offered.

"No," Piper said impatiently, wiping her right cheek with a flour-covered hand. "I don't need any help. I've got to do this on my own. And, Fin, you better keep that frog out of my way."

"Ten minutes gone," Milla said. Piper cringed, put her head down, and got back to work.

Finley squatted in a corner of the kitchen, tapping the frog's cage while Piper whipped the sweet potatoes together with honey, vanilla, a bit of heavy cream, and some spices. "This will be the first of three tart fillings," she explained to her audience. Then she made a second mixture using the sweet peas, and a third with the peach-banana. She dipped the end of a spoon into each of her mixtures after every ingredient she added, testing to see if she'd successfully turned the baby foods into something delicious and rich.

"Not sweet enough," she announced after a mouthful of the pea filling. Making a face after tasting the peach-banana, she declared, "Gross. Too sweet. Needs a savory undertone." She offered her friends a bit of the sweet potato filling, saying, "This one's good, yeah?"

Just as she had begun to ladle her fillings into

the center of her tart crusts, Mariana held up her hand and yelled, "Stop! Time for your next surprise challenge."

Piper clapped, bouncing from one foot to the other. "I'm ready."

"From now on, you can only use your Bunsen burner for cooking stuff. No oven, stove, or microwave."

Piper grinned. "Interesting challenge," she said, laughing. "Can I also use the tripod, so I have a flat surface to cook stuff over the flame?"

"Uh," Mari said, turning to the other girls for consensus. They all nodded. "Sure."

"I like this challenge," Piper said. "A true test of mixing food and science. Not sure how I'm going to bake my tart crusts without the oven, so . . . I might need to change the plan. Good. Change is good." She chewed her lip. After a moment, she nodded and then threw herself back into her (one-handed) work. "If I could modify the crust dough in some way that I could cook

these as dumplings in a boiling water bath . . . ,"
she muttered to herself, poking at the soft white
rounds of dough. She opened drawers, pulled out
her Bunsen burner and a heatproof mat, and then
started to set up the tripod.

"You're not allowed to light your burner without telling Dad," Finley helpfully pointed out.
Piper glared at her sister, scowling when she saw
that Finley had taken the frog out of its cage and
was rubbing its rubbery back with her thumb.
Finley grinned at her and said, *"Purrr purrrr
purrrrrrr."*

"Yeah," Piper snapped. "I know I need to
tell Dad." For the past few years, Piper had been
allowed to use her lab (also known as the kitchen)
without parental supervision, as long as someone
knew what she was working on, and assuming
there was a parent home. The Bunsen burner was
so powerful and flammable, however, that her
parents insisted they be within arm's reach when
she was lighting and using it.

Suddenly, Piper realized that if her dad got a full-time job in an office, she wouldn't be allowed to do experiments in her lab after school. A wave of disappointment washed over her, and she was momentarily distracted. For a second, she forgot what she'd been doing. "Focus," she muttered out loud. "Come on, Piper."

"Ten minutes left," Milla told her. "You've got this!"

Piper raced around the kitchen, tasting, stirring, mixing, and pounding—still with only one hand. She didn't want to call her dad out of his office to light the Bunsen burner until everything was ready to go—and she still had more prep to do. Even without the burner on, Piper could already feel little beads of sweat running down her temples. She flung her hat to the floor. She was almost always cold, so she wore something on her head pretty much all year round—but at the moment, the stress of finishing was making her sweat.

"Do you want some help?" Milla offered, sensing her friend's panic. "If you tell me what to do, I could be an extra set of hands. Four minutes left . . ."

"No," Piper muttered. *If I can't handle this practice run,* she reasoned, *what am I going to do on the day of filming?* "I don't want help. I can do it myself."

But there was so much to do, Piper realized, and so little time. Piper felt *stressed* in her lab, for the first time ever. Looking at the pile of ingredients, and thinking about how much was left to do . . . *ugh!* She almost felt the way she did during tests at school. Like the jumble and mess was too much for her to make sense of, and it would be impossible to figure anything out before her time was up.

"Piper, let me help you," Milla urged again. She stood up and came around the counter. "I can just clean some of this stuff up, so you have more room to wor—"

Milla stopped talking as Piper, who was carrying a cookie sheet filled with tart crust dough, bumped into her. Piper screamed as little dough rounds flew into the air.

Milla stepped backward, tripping over Finley. To avoid crushing the little girl, Milla threw her weight to the side and crashed into the kitchen island. Her elbow hit the tripod, sending it toppling into a bowl of sweet potato filling. The orange mixture fell to the floor and splattered all over the kitchen.

Meanwhile, the frog—which had previously been safely tucked inside Finley's closed palm—took its chance to jump to freedom. As Finley fell over, the frog squirmed out of her fist and leaped into the air. "Get it!" Finley wailed.

All six girls raced into action, chasing after the little critter as it hopped and zoomed around the kitchen. Cooking utensils and tart filling flew in all directions. The frog zipped back and forth across the room like the ball in a pinball machine.

Every time someone got close to catching it, the frog bounced off in the other direction.

"Got it!" Ruby finally cried. She had trapped the frog under a pea-splattered bowl. She slowly lifted the bowl off the floor and then cradled the escaped pet between her palms. It was covered in Piper's sticky pea filling.

As soon as the frog had been rinsed off and returned safely to its cage, Finley crawled around the kitchen island to investigate. Then she crouched down on all fours and started to lap up a spill with her tongue. "Meow like it!"

Mari giggled. "I've got to say: The tarts don't *look* pretty, but at least you know your creation tastes good."

"Yeah." Zahra nodded, trying to hold back a laugh. "The plating in this challenge definitely could have used a little work. Something to think about for next time."

"I'm *so* sorry, Piper," Milla said softly. "I was trying to help."

"It's okay," Piper said, surveying the kitchen. She mustered up a smile to show her friend she wasn't upset with her. "This wasn't your fault. I shouldn't have lost my cool." One by one, she picked up the rounds of dough and tossed them in the trash. "But I'm pretty sure we could call this surprise challenge a total fail."

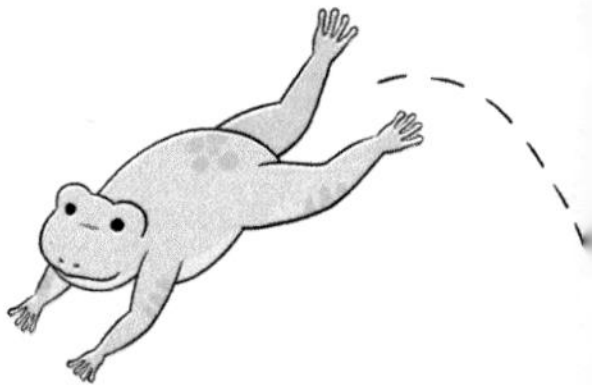

Mariana

Even though I love swimming (and I'm pretty good at it), I don't always <u>love</u> it. I guess that probably doesn't make any sense. I love the way I feel after I win a race or get a personal best. I love that swimming is such an important activity to my family. I love hanging out with my friends at meets and during practice.

But sometimes, I'm not sure if swimming is my passion, you know? Being with Piper in her kitchen is amazing, because she gets so excited and energetic. I like watching her cook and experiment with stuff, because she's obviously very passionate about food science. It's easy to see that she loves it. I don't know if I have that same feeling about swimming.

There was never any question about me joining the swim team (it's something every Sanchez does). My parents are swimmers, my older sisters are all swimmers, so naturally I'm a swimmer, too. I didn't ever say, hey, I really want to join swim team! When I turned five, I just started going to practices and it became my thing.

Here's where Ariel and I are most alike: She was raised in this royal family, and everyone had these expectations for who and what she would become because of the family she was born into. But Ariel secretly had other interests, different stuff she wanted to explore and try out before she was ready to settle down and accept the life her dad planned for her, right? That's me, too.

You asked us to write about a fear, and this is one of mine: I'm afraid to tell my parents that I might not want to be a swimmer anymore. Or not as much of a swimmer, anyway. Right now, I go to five or six practices a week, which doesn't really leave a lot of time for trying other stuff. I guess I kind of want a chance to see if there's something else I love, like theater, or maybe piano or cello, or even another sport. I want to find something that makes me as happy as Piper is when she's cooking and creating and testing stuff. (Zahra has her art, Ruby has soccer, and Milla loves writing.)

I don't know what that something is, but I wish I could explore a little bit and find out. Like Ariel, I kind of want to trade my fins for something else for a while, and just see what happens.

Someday, maybe. A girl can dream, right?

7
SCHOOL SLUMP

"Quiz me." Piper thrust a sheet of paper at Finley while the two sisters were walking to school a few days later. "Please."

Finley took the paper from her sister and squinted at it. "What—*crrrrrk*—is this? *Ribbit*." She did a little frog hop, practicing her new animal moves for the week. Ever since she'd spent the weekend caring for her class pet, Finley had been obsessed with frogs. Piper, not so much.

"My spelling word list," Piper told her sister. "We have a test this morning, and I didn't have time to study."

Finley croaked and hopped. "*Crrrrrrk.*"

"That's not one of my words," Piper said with a smile.

"*Ribbit,*" Finley said.

"That's not a spelling word, either," Piper said. "This is serious, Fin. If I get more than five wrong, I have to bring the test home for mom and dad to sign." She still hadn't shown her parents her terrible math quiz. By some miracle, Mr. Mohan hadn't asked about it yet—but if she had to take a bad spelling test home, too, she knew she was in for some serious trouble.

Piper's usually chill parents had both been on edge lately. Her dad had said he was feeling tense because job interviews are very stressful. But Piper had accidentally overheard her mom and dad talking in the kitchen the night before (when she was supposed to be in bed), and she now knew it was bigger than that. They had talked about money, and how it would really help a lot if her dad could get more work. Unfortunately, while she was eavesdropping, she had overheard something she wished she hadn't. Her dad was interviewing for a full-time job with one of his clients. And the company's offices were in Chicago!

If her dad got the job, her family would have to *move*. The thought of that made Piper want to throw up. She just had to hope he wasn't seriously considering the job.

"Why didn't you study?" Finley asked, frog-hopping over every crack in the sidewalk.

"That doesn't matter," Piper lied. The truth was, she had tried to distract herself from what she had overheard by watching old episodes of *The Future of Food*. She'd stayed up way too late and had forgotten all about the test. "What matters is I'm studying now."

"Okay," Finley said. "I can't read the first word on this list. How do you say C-O-N-T-I-N-E-N-T?"

Piper rolled her eyes. " 'Continent,' " she said,

grabbing the paper out of her sister's hands. "You can't read any of these words, can you?"

"Nope-si-do," Finley said proudly. *"Ribbit!"*

"Forget it."

"How's everyone's week going so far?" Ms. Bancroft asked later that afternoon in advisory group.

"Honestly?" Piper grumbled. "Mine's been crummy."

Ms. Bancroft frowned. "Fill me in."

Piper quickly told Ms. Bancroft about the surprise challenge practice fiasco over the weekend—the one-handed cooking, the baby food, and the Bunsen burner. Though Piper was still depressed about how the challenge had turned out, the other club members didn't seem as bothered by it. Her friends kept cutting in, adding details and humor to the story. Hearing their take on the whole thing helped cheer her up a bit.

"I love that Finley pulled the frog into the kitchen on a skateboard!" Ruby said, giggling. "She acted like it was a dog on a leash."

"Ms. Bancroft, there were mounds of baby food pea goop *everywhere!*" Zahra laughed. "Piper's kitchen looked like a Jackson Pollock painting." The other girls looked confused, so Zahra explained, "He's an artist who threw paint at his canvases."

"It wasn't just the kitchen that looked like a splotchy canvas; my *socks* were covered in sweet potato!" Mari added.

"We should have had Chip come in to lick it up," Milla said. "It took forever to clean the kitchen after I knocked everything over."

Piper nodded. "The whole thing felt a little *too* much like *The Princess and the Frog*, Ms. B. Everything was going along just fine, then—*poof!*—a frog appears and makes a mess of everything."

Ms. Bancroft laughed along with the rest of the group. "It sounds like you got some good practice overcoming obstacles. A real-life application of this week's journal assignment," she pointed out. "Do you feel more prepared for the competition?"

Piper's smile faded. "Not really," she admitted. After a long pause, she said, "Honestly, what really bothers me is that I kind of panicked under all that pressure. I lost my cool, and that's when everything fell apart. I'm nervous I'm going to choke when the Kitchen Wizard starts throwing surprise challenges at me. I'm pretty sure I'm a good cook and a great food scientist. And I *know* I want to win. But what if that's not enough?"

"No," Ruby said forcefully. "You've got this."

"Something all of you should always remember is that confidence is an important part of achieving your dreams," Ms. Bancroft said. "You're driven, you're obviously very talented, and you know what you want. It makes sense that you're nervous. But, Piper, you and I—and the rest of the Daring Dreamers—know you deserve this opportunity. I'm sure you also know you'll do a wonderful job."

Piper shrugged, trying to muster up a smile. "Usually, I feel like I can do just about anything I put my mind to if I work hard enough. But lately—" She cut herself off, shaking her head. She didn't need to broadcast her failures. That wasn't going to solve anything. "Never mind."

Ms. Bancroft said softly, "What else is bothering you?"

"We're here to help," Milla offered.

Piper tugged at a loose piece of thread on her hat. She looked around at the circle of friends, who were all waiting for her to say something. "I just . . ." She took a deep breath. *Where to start?* she thought. She opened her mouth, and everything spilled out. "I'm failing math, even though I'm working really hard to get caught up," she began. "I'm afraid I'm going to screw up in front of the whole world on television," she added quickly. "My dad is looking for a full-time job, and one of the companies he's interviewing at is in Chicago. I *don't* want to move."

"Wait," Milla said, stopping her. "*What?*"

Piper shrugged, then briefly told the group about the conversation she'd overheard between her parents the night before.

"So you might move?" Mariana said. She glanced at Milla, who looked like she was close to tears after hearing this news. Zahra, who was sitting next to Milla, draped an arm across her shoulders and squeezed.

Piper threw her hands up in the air. "I don't know what's going to happen, but now I feel like I *have* to win *The Future of Food*! Ten thousand dollars is enough money that maybe my dad wouldn't have to find a full-time job right away. And he for sure wouldn't have to hurry up and take one in Chicago. Right?" As soon as she said all this aloud, Piper felt her stomach unknot, just

the slightest bit. It did feel good to talk about her worries, even if no one could help her fix anything.

Ms. Bancroft nodded. "I can see why you might feel the money would be a big help," she said. "It is a large prize. But you're putting too much pressure on yourself. I can't speak for your parents, but I feel fairly certain they wouldn't want you worrying about your family's finances. You have a lot of other things going on." She paused. "What's this about math? That's one place where I *can* assist you."

Piper hung her head. "It's nothing," she muttered. "I'll figure it out if I just keep working on it. Spelling, too. I obviously just need to study harder, and I'll be fine."

"No, that's *not* true," Milla said forcefully. Everyone turned to look at her. Milla was usually fairly soft-spoken, but she suddenly sounded a lot like Ruby. "You are being one hundred percent Piper right now. You can't do everything on your own! If you're having trouble with math, you have to ask for help. You *know* that. Staring at your math problems without understanding anything is *not* going to help you solve them." She shook her head. "Even Tiana figured out that she had to ask for help—from a trumpet-playing alligator and a *firefly,* no less. You could have asked *me.* I'm *great* at math, remember?" She crossed her arms and waited for Piper to respond.

Piper blinked and let out a big sigh. Then she unzipped her backpack, pulled out the failed math quiz, and handed it to Milla. With a tiny shrug, she whispered, "Help?"

Milla

One of the things I've always loved about Belle is her kindness and compassion toward others. She looked past the Beast's scary outside to find his warm heart.

I often worry about how people will react to my scar when they meet me. So, like Belle, I try to go out of my way to be kind and treat everyone with respect, with the hope that others will see past the marks on my face and get to know me as a person. Sometimes you can't see what's going on with people on the inside (how someone looks usually has nothing to do with what's going on under the surface of their skin). You never know what kinds of things people are dealing with in their personal lives.

Like Piper these past few weeks! I really wish she had told me she was having so much trouble in school. I can't believe she's fallen

so far behind. She always makes it seem like everything is totally fine, but it's not. And I'm sad she didn't feel like she could talk to me about it. I thought we were best friends and could talk about anything, but I guess she felt like she had to hide her problems from me. Same goes for her dad's job interview in Chicago. I wish she had told me about all the things she's been worrying about so I could have been there for her.

You asked us to talk about one of our greatest fears in our journals this week, and here's one of mine: that Piper will move! She's been my best friend since we started elementary school, and she's one of the only people who really, truly knows me. Other than my moms, she's the only person who I've ever felt comfortable opening up to. Piper has always been able to bring out the brave and fearless version of me that I usually only write about in my stories (like at the fifth-grade overnight)! Having her there with me made that big adventure a lot less scary. I don't know what I'd do without her in my life every day.

For a little while, I guess I was feeling kind of mad at her for not telling me about her dad's job stuff and her school troubles. But now I'm just sad and afraid. I don't know what I can do other than be here to support her and help her when she needs me. I guess I'll remind her that she can always tell me the truth, and I'll never judge her, no matter what. I'm pretty sure Belle would tell me that's what friends are for.

8
FAT TESTS AND MATH EXPERIMENTS

"How did your interview go today?" Piper asked her dad on Wednesday afternoon, trying to sound casual. Deep down, she couldn't help hoping it had gone terribly. She had peeked at the calendar on his desk that morning and noticed that he'd had a video call scheduled with the company in Chicago.

"It went really well," her dad said, settling onto a stool at the kitchen counter. "I'm excited about possibly doing more work with them."

"Oh," Piper said. She waited to see if he would say more. Was he *ever* going to tell her,

Finley, and Dan that he was interviewing for a job in *Chicago*? She glared at her dad, but he didn't notice. He was too busy looking down at his phone, probably shopping for new houses in a new city or Googling "ways to ruin your kids' lives." Or something like that.

Once again, Piper reassured herself that it was totally fair that she was hiding her horrible math quiz from her parents. After all, they were keeping a massive secret from her! Somehow she had managed to squeak by with only four wrong on that week's spelling test, so at least she didn't have to hide a *second* test from them.

"Whaddya working on?" her dad asked, finally glancing up from his phone.

"I'm making cookies," Piper said grumpily. "I've been trying to figure out how different fats affect the shape, texture, and crunch level in baked goods."

"I'd be happy to evaluate the results," her dad said, rubbing his belly. "That is a job I can truly say I'm qualified for." He waggled his eyebrows and gave her a goofy grin.

Piper refused to smile back. She just stirred and stewed. "We'll see how far I get. I need to start dinner soon."

"You want any help?" her dad offered. "I finished up my work for the day."

"Nope," Piper said stiffly. "I'm on it." For the past week, Piper had cooked dinner for her family every single night—partly because the kitchen was always a disaster from her experiments-in-progress, but also partly because her dad had been working a lot more than usual. Between preparing for his interviews and another big project deadline, he had been working late into the evening most nights.

Piper didn't mind spending extra time in the kitchen. It was great practice. But the past week had given her a pretty good idea of how things would be if both her parents were working full-time—busy and chaotic. Between her brother's sports practices, her sister's dance classes, their volunteer shifts at Helping Hands, and both of her parents being at work from eight in the morning until six at night, their life was going to be really nutty. Piper felt ready to step up and take on more responsibility around the house, but it was still hard to think about things changing.

"Do you have homework?" her dad asked. "I don't want you spending more time in the kitchen if it's keeping you from your schoolwork."

"A little," Piper muttered.

"When Dan was in fifth grade, he had at least a half an hour of math homework each night. Seems like they're going easier on you this year," he noted.

"I'm not Dan," Piper snapped.

"Whoa," her dad said, his eyes widening. "That's not what I meant."

"If you expect me to be just like him," Piper grumbled, "you're going to be disappointed."

Piper's dad rapped on the counter with his knuckles. "Piper . . ." He waited for her to look at him. "I do not expect you to be just like Dan. You know that, right?"

"I'm never going to be as smart as him. No matter how hard I work and how much time I spend on my homework, Dan will always be the smart and sporty one." She crossed her arms defiantly. "Finley will always be the funny, adorable

one. I'll always be the messy middle one."

Her dad laughed, but Piper didn't find what she'd said all that funny. She was being serious! Piper glared down at her bowl as she mixed the cookie dough. She glanced up at her dad briefly, her mouth set in a scowl. Her dad finally realized she wasn't laughing along and said gently, "You're different kids. You came packaged with different skills."

"And obviously my skills aren't math related," Piper snapped. She and Milla had spent some time working on math problems during recess that day. But no matter how many times or different ways Milla explained things to her, Piper just couldn't seem to get it. Milla kept reminding her to take it slow—telling her that it wasn't a race— but Piper *hated* taking things slow. She was a slow reader, a slow writer, and now she was supposed to go slow in math, too? It wasn't fair; slow was boring! "I'm never going to get straight As, no matter how hard I work."

Her dad shook his head. "We don't *expect* you to get straight As. Your mom and I just want you to put in your best effort. You know that, don't you, Piper?"

"I guess," Piper grumbled.

As if on cue, smarty-pants Dan sauntered into the kitchen, slapping his sweaty soccer shin guards on the counter. Then he peeled off his stinky jersey and tossed that on the counter as well. He grabbed an apple out of the fridge and took a big spoonful of cookie dough out of one of Piper's bowls.

"Ahem," Piper said, flicking Dan's shin guards onto the floor. "Keep your stench out of my lab."

Dan grinned at her, lifted his arm, and waved his armpit in front of her face.

"You're totally disgusting," Piper said, swatting at him. At least Dan wasn't perfect in *every* way, she told herself.

★★★

Later that night, after the dinner dishes had been washed and Piper had shared the results of her cookie experiment with her family (everyone agreed that the batch made with coconut oil was the tastiest and most interesting), she settled in at the dining room table to work on her math. Again.

Finley slid into the seat beside her and began drawing a picture of a scientist in a lab. Piper was happy to see that the scientist looked an awful lot like *her*! Piper's parents were both reading in the living room, but Dan was lurking around the dining room table, watching her.

"What?" Piper asked after it was clear Dan wasn't going anywhere.

"Can I help?" Dan asked quietly. "I'm pretty good at math."

"I know you are," Piper said. "We *all* know you are."

Dan sighed and rolled his eyes. "Let me help you," he whispered, glancing over his shoulder.

Piper could tell he was speaking softly so their parents wouldn't hear him. Speaking even more quietly, he said, "If Mom and Dad find out about the failed quiz you're hiding from them, there's no way they're going to let you go on *The Future of Food.*"

Piper gaped at him. "How—" she began. "How do you know about that?"

"I saw it the other night." He tapped his temple. "I see things. And I'm your brother, and I don't want you to screw this up for yourself."

"*Ribbit,*" Finley bellowed.

Piper considered his offer. Dan was a math genius. He was annoyingly brilliant at *every* subject. It seemed she was . . . well, not.

Dan plopped into the seat across from her. He looked her straight in the eye and said, "I'll make you a deal. I help you come up with strategies for your word problem unit, and in exchange, you bake me and the soccer team cookies every day for a week. And when you win *The Future of*

Food, you buy me a new soccer bag with part of the money you win. Deal?"

Piper laughed. "*When* I win?" she asked. "I think you mean *if* I win."

"Nope," Dan said. "I mean *when*."

Piper appreciated the offer—and her brother's compliment. She didn't want to take help, but it seemed like she didn't have much of a choice. Sometimes, getting a little help was the only way to succeed. "Deal."

"Here's the thing you have to remember," Dan said softly. "You've never been *bad* at math. You're obviously good with numbers and calculations if you can follow and make up your own recipes. There's precision in science and cooking, right?" He propped his elbows on the table and fixed Piper with a serious look. Then he went on, "Math is a lot like science—it's going to take you some time and practice to figure out the formula that works for you. We'll look at your homework a few different ways. We can break it down, step by step, and see where you're running into problems. Like an experiment."

When he put it that way, Piper suddenly felt hopeful. "An experiment? You can do experiments with math?"

"There's no one way to look at equations," Dan assured her. "We'll find the way that works for you. I promise."

9
PRACTICE MAKES
NOT-QUITE-PERFECT

The week leading up to Piper's appearance on *The Future of Food* flew by. She and Dan worked on her math together every night. Dan hung out with Piper in the kitchen while she tested different recipes and techniques, and together they had come up with a game where Piper was required to solve a math problem correctly in order to win her next ingredient or tool. (Finley helped out by swiping tools and ingredients. Then she presented them game-show-style when Piper got a correct answer.) It felt a little like the Kitchen Wizard's surprise challenges, so Piper actually stopped dreading their tutoring sessions. She didn't *enjoy* taking orders and advice from her brother, but their time together wasn't as awful as she had expected.

Though her parents still hadn't said anything about her dad's interviews with the Chicago company, Piper knew he was still talking to them about the job. She had seen another call with the same company written down in his calendar. Her dad's desk was out in the open for anyone to see, so Piper had figured snooping a little wasn't technically wrong.

One night, after Finley had gone to bed, Piper decided to tell her brother about the Chicago interviews. She figured talking the situation out with Dan might help. The two of them discussed it, and Dan agreed that Piper winning a $10,000 prize would probably be a big help. He was sure it would be enough money so their dad could wait to find a job closer to home. Now Piper felt even more pressure to win.

Because she knew the prize money would mean a lot to her family, Piper had turned into a nervous wreck. "I hate to say it, but prepping for *The Future of Food* is starting to feel like doing math homework," she confessed to Dan on Thursday night, two days before the big event. "It seems like no matter how hard I practice, I'll never be completely ready. What if I screw up?"

"The goal isn't perfection, Piper," Dan said, frowning at her. "It's about getting a little better, one step at a time. You're the one who always tells me that, in the kitchen, being perfect doesn't matter. You learn from your errors, and then move on knowing a little more than you did before. It's exactly the same thing with math. Right?"

Piper *had* said that. But it sounded crazy now. She was supposed to go on TV, on a show that millions of people would watch, and there was still so much more she had to learn!

By the time Friday rolled around, she was a

ball of nerves and energy. Every time she picked up a cooking tool or thought about another gadget she needed to test out or learn how to use, she felt her breath quicken and her heart start to race. What if she didn't win? What a waste of time all of this would have been!

"Piper?" Mr. Mohan said, calling her name just as they were being dismissed for recess on Friday. "Can I speak with you for a moment?"

She hung back as her classmates raced toward the playground. She glanced at her math notebook, knowing full well that her teacher was going to ask her about that failed quiz. It had been folded up in the back of her notebook for almost two weeks now. She had always known she couldn't hide it from her parents forever.

"Our next unit test is coming up in math," Mr. Mohan said. "I wanted to check in with you to see how things have been going over the past few weeks. Do you need any extra help, or—"

"I think I'm ready for the next test," Piper

blurted out, hoping it was true. "I've been working really hard, and I know I'll do better than I did on the last quiz."

Mr. Mohan nodded. "I'm still waiting for a parent's signature on that last quiz," he said quietly. "Have you shared it with your mom or dad yet?"

Piper chewed her lip. "Not yet," she said slowly, an idea forming in her mind. "But, Mr. Mohan, I have a proposal for you."

Her teacher laughed. "Why am I not surprised?"

"How do you feel about me retaking the last quiz?" she said. "You can test me with different problems, but make it a quiz on the same basic material. If I improve my score, we agree that I don't have to show that bad quiz score to my parents." She smiled hopefully at him. "I'd like a chance to show you I'm learning from my mistakes. I don't know if I'll get a perfect score, but I've been studying and practicing problems at home. I've figured out some strategies that help me break down these story problems. I *know* I can do better than last time. Isn't that what matters? That I'm learning and improving?"

Mr. Mohan said nothing for a long moment. Then he nodded. "That seems totally fair," he said. "I'd like to see if you're improving and moving in the right direction."

Piper thrust out her hand to shake on it. "Then it sounds like we've got a deal."

10
RECIPE FOR WINNING

"I brought you something," Piper told her fellow Daring Dreamers later that day. She pulled a plastic container out of her backpack and popped open the lid. "I finally finished the baby food surprise challenge. I was mad at myself for giving up last weekend when everything went wrong. So I got three new jars of baby food and finished the challenge last night. My family ate all the sweet potato and fruit tarts before I could pack them up to share, but I had a few of the mashed pea ones left over. They're actually pretty good."

"It's awesome that you gave it another go,"

Ruby said. She sniffed one of the pea-green-colored balls. "But I've got to be honest, Piper. These snacks look . . . creepy."

"Looks can be deceiving," Piper said, wiggling her eyebrows. "Remember, I had to cook everything using my Bunsen burner, so they're not going to be super pretty. Taste before you judge." She glanced at Milla. "No dairy or nuts."

Milla took a timid bite, grateful as always that her pal was mindful of her food allergies. "It's so sweet!" Milla said, surprised by the flavor of the odd-colored ball. The dough was soft and light, and the filling inside was creamy and unexpectedly citrusy. "How did you do that?"

"It's all about mixing the right ingredients," Piper said, beaming. "Science, my friend. Food science."

"So how are you feeling about your big day tomorrow?" Ms. Bancroft asked. "Are you ready?"

"I guess?" Piper said, shrugging. "You're all coming to watch, right?"

"I wouldn't miss it," Ms. Bancroft said with a smile.

The other girls nodded. "My mom and Mari's dad are driving everyone there," Milla told her. "We're supposed to be at the studio by noon?"

"Yup," Piper answered. Then she shook her head. "I just hope I win. Otherwise, this is all for nothing. The stress, nerves, hard work . . ."

Ms. Bancroft gave her a funny look. "Is that really how you feel?" she asked.

Piper shrugged. "It's ten thousand dollars, Ms. B. I definitely want to win."

"But this experience is about so much more than the prize money," Ms. Bancroft reminded her. "When you dream big, it's important to savor every step of the journey, and not just focus on the end goal." Ms. Bancroft paused, and then said quietly, "Let me tell you a story. It's about me, when I was around your age."

Piper and the other girls listened intently. Ms. Bancroft rarely told them much about herself.

"The summer I turned twelve, I was sent to live with my grandparents, who I'd only met a few times in my life, while my parents sorted through some things at home," Ms. Bancroft began. "As soon as I got to their house, I decided it was going to be a miserable two months. I started counting the days until I could go home again.

"I moped around on the couch every day, watching movies and wishing the summer would hurry up and end. I'd been sent to my grandparents' house against my will, and I was determined to make things difficult for everyone. I was a pretty unpleasant kid, to be honest." She laughed.

"Sounds like you were a real delight," Mari said, giggling.

"My grandparents didn't own a lot of movies, but they did have *Snow White* and *Sleeping Beauty,* which I enjoyed. I watched both movies a hundred times that summer. I spent hours dreaming about how great it would be if I could flee my grandparents' stuffy house and live out in the woods with a pack of dwarves or a fairy godmother for company. I envied both of those princesses, because their lives seemed so much better than mine," Ms. Bancroft explained.

"The grass is always greener in someone else's yard, right?" Zahra agreed. Piper had heard people use that saying before but had never really known what it meant. Now she got it.

"I sometimes heard other kids who lived in my grandparents' neighborhood playing outside," Ms. Bancroft continued, "but I didn't know any of them, and frankly, I didn't really want to know them. They weren't *my* friends, and I knew I was leaving at the end of August—so why bother?"

"Ms. B!" Piper said, giggling. "You had a *bad*-itude."

"I know," Ms. Bancroft said,

laughing along with her. "I didn't make things easy on my poor grandparents." She held up a finger and said, "But then one day, I was watching *Sleeping Beauty* and started to realize that she and Snow White and I were more alike than I'd ever realized. Both Aurora and Snow White were living away from their homes, Snow White with a houseful of strangers and Aurora with temporary guardians . . . and yet they had both figured out how to make the most of the situation they were in. Watching their stories helped me realize that I could be mopey and whiny and complain about being away from home and spend the whole summer waiting for it to end . . . *or* I could make the most of it and enjoy the adventure. That was a big turning point for me."

Piper loved hearing Ms. Bancroft's story, but she didn't understand what this had to do with her or her experience on *The Future of Food*.

Ms. Bancroft went on, "I asked the five of you to write about obstacles and fears in a previous journal assignment for a reason. I hope you remember that you can face challenges and difficult situations head-on and come out stronger on the other side—or you can let them knock you down." She nodded at Piper. "Tiana had big dreams, but she had to overcome all kinds of obstacles to achieve them. And just like you, Piper, she refused to give up. Her perseverance and hard work helped her to achieve those dreams. As long as you're still enjoying yourself and making progress toward fulfilling your big dreams, then no matter what happens tomorrow," she said with a smile, "you've already won."

11
THE FUTURE OF FOOD

On Saturday morning, Piper set her alarm for six. But at five-thirty on the dot, her eyes popped open and she flew out of bed. After a quick shower, she pulled on the loose navy blue pants and pale yellow top Zahra had helped her pick out for her big day. Then she wrestled her hair into braids and, using green pipe cleaners for support, twisted the braids into two lopsided buns, one on each side of her head. Her hair reminded Piper of rainbow cinnamon buns—Zahra had promised the silly and whimsical design would help her look the part of creative chef.

No matter what she looked like, she felt comfortable, confident, and one hundred percent *Piper*. She was ready to take on *The Future of Food*.

Contestants had been told to arrive at the studio by nine. Her parents were both coming early with her. Finley and Dan were going to ride to the studio with Milla's mom so they wouldn't have to sit around all morning waiting for the filmed portion of the competition to begin. Piper was excited to have some alone time with her parents. In a family of five, that didn't happen very often.

Milla called a few minutes after seven to wish her luck and remind her that they would all be cheering for her. "I don't know if we'll get to see you before filming starts," Milla said. "So just pretend we're all giving you big hugs before you go onstage, okay?" Piper was grateful to have such great friends.

As Piper and her parents drove to the set, the

three of them chatted about nothing in particular. It was obvious her parents were both trying to keep Piper's mind off the competition, and she was grateful for the distraction. Still, the drive felt like it took forever—but they pulled into the parking lot at ten minutes to nine.

Piper was grabbing the car door handle when her mom reached into the backseat and placed a hand on Piper's leg. "Can I just say how proud we are of you?" she said. "You're going to be fantastic today."

"Thanks," Piper said, smiling. "I'm proud of me, too."

Her parents laughed. "You are really something, Piper," her dad added, twisting around to face her in the backseat. "Fearless, smart, and confident. That's quite a combination. I'm not sure where you got your kitchen and science smarts, but it's always fun watching you do your thing."

"For real?" Piper said. "But it's just food

science. It's not like this is a soccer tournament, or a math competition, or one of Finley's super-cute dance recitals."

"It's not *just* food science!" her mom said, a strange look flashing across her face. "What you do in the kitchen is amazing, Piper. I hope you know we both really admire your creativity. And what you do at Helping Hands, not to mention the way you contribute with our family dinners, is really cool."

"But . . . ," Piper said, looking from her mom to her dad. "Sometimes I wonder if it's easier for you guys to be proud of Dan and Finley. I mean, Dan wins all those trophies, prizes, and certificates. And Finley is, well, *Finley.* I'm just the boring, nonathletic, not-so-smart leftover."

"Oh, Piper," her mom said, shaking her head. "That's not what you think, is it?"

"Sorta," Piper confessed. "I really want to win today so I finally have proof that I'm the best at something, too. Sometimes, I feel like all I ever do is make a huge mess of things."

"That could not be further from the truth," her dad said firmly. "One of the things I love most about you is that you forge your own path. You question things, you look at problems differently than other people, and you solve them in your own way. You're the best at being *you*."

"I am certainly good at that," Piper agreed. Then she frowned. "But what if I *don't* win today? The ten thousand dollars—"

"You can't think about that," her mom said.

"But . . . ," Piper began. "But don't we need the money so Dad doesn't have to take that job in Chicago?"

Her parents glanced at each other. "What job in Chicago?" her dad asked.

"You were interviewing with that company you do work for in Chicago, right? For a full-time gig?"

"I've been talking about doing more work for them, yes," her dad said. "They did offer me a full-time position, but I told them I can only consider it if it's a work-from-home position."

"So then we wouldn't move to Chicago?" Piper asked hopefully.

"No one's moving to Chicago," her mom said. "My job is here, your school is here, your friends are here. But your dad is going to pick up more work no matter what."

"I'm bored," her dad said, shrugging. "I've been a busy stay-at-home dad for years, and without any of you hanging around during the day, I'm going a little crazy. I *want* to work more."

"Even if I win ten thousand dollars?"

Her dad nodded. "I'm looking for more work because I like to be busy, and I *miss* working full-time. I know it will change some things, but I want to challenge myself. And just to be clear, if you win ten thousand dollars, that's *your* ten thousand dollars—to save for college."

"If I *don't* win, is college off the table?" Piper asked, tilting her head.

"No," her mom said. "And this is not the time to have that discussion. It's time for us to go inside." She patted Piper's knee. "Are you ready to show the Kitchen Wizard who's going to rule the future of food?"

Piper hopped out of the car. "I sure am."

When the three Andelmans stepped inside the enormous warehouse set, a tall, thin woman holding a clipboard rushed over to them. "Welcome!" the lady said. "I'm Lydia, one of the production assistants. You must be Piper?"

Piper nodded. She could feel the buns on each side of her head bobbing along. Somehow, because the buns had been Zahra's idea, it almost felt as if Zahra were standing and nodding beside her—and that made her feel a little less nervous. "Piper Andelman," she said, thrusting her hand toward Lydia.

"We're excited to have you on the show today—your audition video was super fun, and we love your creative spark," Lydia said, shaking Piper's hand. "I'm going to show you around the set, give you some time to check out your workstation, then walk you through your schedule. Sound good?"

"Sounds good," Piper said. From where she stood, she could see hundreds of lights set up

around an industrial kitchen set. There were dozens of official-looking people bustling around. Piper craned her neck, trying to spot the other contestants.

Squinting, she gazed across the room. She noticed someone wearing chef whites on the far side of the set. The man's handlebar mustache had been waxed into two delicate curlicues over his top lip, and his face was immediately recognizable. "Is that . . . ," she began, looking to Lydia for confirmation, "Arlo VanDries?"

Lydia smiled. "Sure is. His son is one of the other contestants on today's episode."

Piper gulped. "Arlo VanDries has a *son*? And I'm competing against him?"

Piper's mom looked at her with a questioning look. "Who is Arlo VanDries?"

Piper sighed. "Only the executive chef of Arlo's Bistro."

"That fancy French restaurant?" her mom said in a voice that was not at all reassuring.

"Like, *Arlo* of Arlo's Bistro?"

"That's the one," Piper answered. She had spent some time the previous summer researching local chefs. Mr. VanDries was the most famous of the bunch. He had been trained by big-name chefs in New York City and spent several years learning even more about French cooking in the south of France. He had won awards! Surely his son knew a few—or a few *million*—things about cooking. "I'm competing against Arlo VanDries's kid," she said quietly. "Who else am I up against?"

"It's a good mix today. You all come from very different backgrounds, which will make for a fun show." Lydia glanced down at her clipboard. "Today we've got Jack VanDries, Frankie Catapano, and you. You'll get to meet them when you go into makeup."

The name Frankie Catapano sounded familiar. As soon as she realized why, Piper's eyes widened. "Frankie of Frankie's FancyCakes?" she asked, hoping she was wrong. "The YouTube star?"

"The one and only," Lydia said with a smile. "Her cake-decorating skills are incredible, aren't they?"

Piper squeaked in agreement. Though she'd known she would be competing against some great chefs, the thought of going up against a YouTube star (whose videos she had been following for over a year!) and a famous chef's son made her stomach clench with nerves. How could she possibly beat either one of them? Was it too late to back out?

"You're going to adore both contestants," Lydia said reassuringly. "Don't let anyone's fame or background intimidate you. And remember that you deserve to be here just as much as anyone."

"Uh-huh," Piper said, gulping.

Lydia patted her on the back and guided her toward the kitchen. "Just try to have fun with today's challenge, and don't be afraid to take some chances. That's what the Kitchen Wizard and today's guest judge will love to see more than anything."

Piper nodded, but she couldn't help wondering what she'd been thinking when she'd sent in her audition video. Then she took a deep breath and forced herself to focus on Lydia's advice, which aligned perfectly with Ms. Bancroft's wise words from the previous afternoon. She had to remember to have *fun* while she was here. It wasn't only about winning; it was about the experience.

Surely she could learn a few things from her competitors. She smiled as another thought popped into her head: maybe her competitors could learn a few things from her, too. "Yep," she told Lydia, her smile widening. "I'm ready to have some serious fun."

Piper

I'm not gonna lie: Stepping onto <u>The Future of Food</u> set was terrifying. There were so many people, lights, and cameras (cooking on TV is nothing like working in my lab). It was super scary at first, but I knew I couldn't let the situation freak me out. I put in a lot of hard work to get a spot on the show, and I definitely deserved to be there just as much as any of the other contestants. They wouldn't have picked me if they didn't think I stood a decent chance of winning, right?

Sure, I had to go up against a famous YouTuber and an even more famous chef's son. So what? I've faced bigger challenges than that. Tiana didn't let the Shadow Man scare her, so I wasn't about to let a couple of kids intimidate me. Tiana figured out how to deal with the obstacles she was up against, and she won in the end. Just like

I've figured out the best ways to deal with my dyslexia and my math challenges . . . with tons of hard work, patience, focus, and help.

Part of what I love about science is dealing with curveballs. It's all about overcoming obstacles big and small. In the lab, I can't control everything (just like in life, I guess?), and it's important to work with whatever challenges are thrown my way.

Speaking of hard work and fighting through challenges . . . Mr. Mohan let me take a makeup math quiz, and I got an 87 percent! That's pretty close to perfect, if I do say so myself. I think Mr. Mohan was a little surprised, but I reminded him that Piper Andelman doesn't go down without a fight. I'm a lot of things (friend, sister, chef, scientist, inventor) but something I'm not? A quitter!

12
THE KITCHEN WIZARD

After spending most of the morning looking over her workstation and checking out all the tools that would be at her disposal during the competition, Piper felt totally comfortable in the space. She had rearranged everything so the knives were to the *left* of her cutting boards (her workstation had been set up for a right-handed person, which would do her no good at all). She also took a few minutes to make sure all her equipment was working correctly and attempted to memorize the whereabouts of supplies in the pantry and fridges.

Around noon, Lydia told her it was time to

clear out of her workstation so the production people could do a sound and lighting check. Piper, Frankie, and Jack were all ushered into a special waiting room filled with snacks and sandwiches and fancy sodas. She gobbled down a sandwich and tried to chat with the other two kids while some guy covered her face in makeup and powder ("So you don't look sickly on camera," Lydia had explained, when Piper protested).

During lunch, she also got to meet that day's guest judge, a friendly guy named Muneet Bakshi. Mr. Bakshi owned an ice cream company, which sounded like one of the best jobs ever. Piper asked him a million questions about how he developed new flavors and how he'd gotten his business started. Mr. Bakshi told her about all the testing and experimenting that happens before a product ever makes it to the grocery store, and then he invited her to visit his product-development lab, to see how it all worked. She couldn't wait!

Piper barely had time to scarf down a brownie

before Lydia rushed her and the other chefs back to the set. She hadn't gotten much time to chat with either Frankie or Jack, since both of them had been busy with makeup, too. But from what Piper could tell, they both seemed pretty nice. Jack was a little standoffish and mostly spent the lunch break with his dad. Frankie had confessed to Piper that she was nervous, too. Knowing she wasn't the only one who felt that way had made Piper feel a whole lot better.

The Kitchen Wizard stopped to say hello and wish them all luck. The show's host seemed really warm and friendly in person, even though she usually came across as super serious (and even slightly scary) during competitions. She was much shorter than Piper had expected, but her sleek black bob and dark-framed glasses looked just like they did on TV. Piper didn't get to say much more than hello, before Arlo VanDries pulled the Kitchen Wizard aside to talk business and refused to let anyone else get a word in.

Once the show's host had made her way onto the set, the three contestants were told to wait behind a low black wall until she called them out. As soon as the cameras were rolling, they would each enter and introduce themselves.

"Two minutes!" someone warned. Piper's whole body was practically buzzing with excitement. Or shaking with nerves . . . she couldn't quite tell which.

Just as a producer called for quiet on the set, Arlo VanDries grabbed his son's shoulders. "Win this," he told Jack in a low, firm voice. "Don't disappoint me."

Jack nodded, but Piper thought he looked like he was going to be sick. Piper and Frankie exchanged a look. *Poor Jack,* Piper thought. Much as she wanted to win, she knew her friends and family would be proud of her, no matter what the outcome.

"Welcome to *The Future of Food*!" The Kitchen Wizard's steely voice echoed through

the studio. "On today's show," she said, "we've brought together three budding kitchen wizards to see if they have what it takes to shape the future of food. Let's bring out our contestants and learn a little more about who's playing my game! First, we have Frankie Catapano, a creative young pastry chef who has earned more than one million YouTube subscribers with her clever cupcake design videos! Welcome, Frankie!"

Piper watched as a production assistant nudged Frankie out from behind the wall. "Hey!" Frankie said, waving. The live audience clapped.

"What makes *you* a kitchen wizard, Frankie?"

"I started playing around with food design when I was about four. I've always loved art, and I love sweets! There's nothing more fun than combining two of my favorite things!"

"We look forward to seeing some of your artistic vision today," the Kitchen Wizard said. "Next up, we have Jack VanDries."

"Bonjour!" Jack said as he stepped out from behind the wall. Piper giggled. Over the course of the morning, Piper had learned that Jack wasn't French (his dad was from Kansas, and Jack was born in New York), but he loved throwing random French phrases into conversation. Jack talked about his dad's culinary school and restaurant background, and his own experience helping out in the kitchen at some of his dad's restaurants.

Finally, it was Piper's turn. "Hi, everyone!" Piper said, waving as she stepped out from behind the wall. She glanced toward the live audience and immediately spotted her family, her friends, and Ms. B clapping and cheering. Behind them, Duck from Helping Hands was waving madly at her—him being there was an exciting surprise! Piper had been instructed not to interact with the crowd, so she didn't wave back. But knowing they were all there, rooting for her, gave her an extra boost of confidence and made her smile even more widely.

The Kitchen Wizard put her hand on Piper's shoulder. "Tell me," she said with a nod. "What makes you a kitchen wizard, Piper?"

"I've always had a lot of questions about food, cooking, and baking," Piper told her, while trying not to stare into the camera looming in front of her. "It started with basic questions: Why do you need baking soda in cookies? That led to more questions: Why doesn't anyone make peanut butter in stick form to make things easier when you're baking? Does that drive anyone else crazy?"

"Yes! It does!" the Kitchen Wizard said,

nodding. "That is a great question, Piper."

Piper grinned. "A love of science inspired me to start doing experiments in the kitchen. Testing to see what happens when you play around with food and different ways of cooking or baking things. I guess I consider myself part scientist, part chef, and that's why I'm here today."

"Wonderful!" the Kitchen Wizard said.

The cameras spun away from Piper, and the Kitchen Wizard introduced Mr. Bakshi. "Now that we've met today's contestants, it's time to find out who will be helping me decide today's winners. Everyone, please welcome Muneet Bakshi, the founder of Yum! Ice Cream Company."

"Good luck, chefs!" Mr. Bakshi said, giving Piper, Frankie, and Jack a thumbs-up. "I'm excited to see what you whip up today. Creativity is the name of the game!"

As soon as everyone had been introduced, the director called, "Cut!" Piper and the others settled in at their workstations while cameras were moved and wires were fiddled with. Production people pushed some set pieces around, and lighting was adjusted. Someone came onto the set to fix the Kitchen Wizard's makeup, and Jack VanDries pulled out a pocket mirror to check his hair.

Piper waved up at her cheering section, squinting as she tried to pick out each of their faces in the crowd. She grinned when she saw that Finley had made a huge sign with GO PIPER! written in glitter. In the row behind her family, she could see Milla, Zahra, Ruby, and Ms. Bancroft talking together. But where was Mariana? Piper scanned the crowd, but her tall friend was nowhere to be found.

Milla noticed Piper looking up at them and mouthed something at her—but she couldn't figure out what Milla was trying to say. The other three Daring Dreamers started gesturing wildly, but Piper still had no idea what they were trying to tell her. Before she could puzzle it out, someone called, "Quiet on the set!"

A voice in the shadows counted down from five. Then the Kitchen Wizard looked to the camera and said, "Let's get cooking!" Piper glanced over at the host, eager to hear what the day's theme would be. Her eyes widened when she saw that the Kitchen Wizard suddenly looked *much* different than she had just a few minutes before. Her chef jacket was torn and ragged, and her face was gray and mottled. She looked creepy, and her tattered outfit reminded Piper of her brother's fifth-grade Halloween zombie costume.

"Today's theme on *The Future of Food* is . . . ," the Kitchen Wizard said with a flourish, "zombie apocalypse!"

13
ZOMBIE APOCALYPSE

Piper smiled. This would be fun! She glanced over at Jack, who looked slightly horrified. Frankie put her hand over her mouth and laughed; Piper could tell idea wheels were already spinning in her mind.

The Kitchen Wizard explained how the challenge would work. "Imagine you are living in a future where zombies have taken over your peaceful world. Each of you must cook a meal using only foods you would find in an emergency shelter. That means canned goods, shelf-stable products, and any other supplies you are lucky enough to find in our zombie-proof hideout." The Kitchen Wizard raised one thin eyebrow and added, "Unfortunately, this means the regular pantry and fridge are off-limits to you today. I am happy to say, however, that you will have access to your oven, stove, spices, and any other tools already in your workstation."

No fresh produce? Piper thought, cringing. *No meat, no herbs, no butter or milk?* Luckily, she had practice working with dietary restrictions when cooking sweets for Milla. This was a bit more restrictive than she was accustomed to, but she'd make it work. Especially if she had spices and tools to work with. It certainly could be a lot worse!

The Kitchen Wizard beckoned for all the contestants to join her in the makeshift emergency shelter that producers had wheeled onto the set. "Bring your baskets, and get ready to shop for supplies. You'll have one hour to make a delicious three-course meal using products you find inside this shelter." She grinned, reminding them, "As always, there will be a few surprises along the way. Zombies are unpredictable, so you never know what might creep up on you during the course of today's challenge!"

Piper and the other chefs stepped inside the small shelter and looked around. Cameras followed the contestants as they scanned the shelves to see what would be available to them. There were tins of preserved meat, a selection of canned soups, shelf-stable cartons of milk and juice, sweetened condensed milk, both dried *and* canned fruits and vegetables, crackers, toaster pastries, cookies, oatmeal packets, bottles of water, tubs of coconut oil, instant macaroni and cheese, and some meat sticks.

There was actually a lot of stuff to choose from, and Piper felt sure she could create something tasty and interesting that would impress the Kitchen Wizard and Mr. Bakshi. Luckily, her friends' baby food challenge had given her some good practice using unusual ingredients! She was also very glad she'd played around with different fats in her cookies that week, since she now felt comfortable using coconut oil instead of butter for her dessert course.

For an appetizer, she could turn crackers into flatbread, using a bit of the coconut oil, cheese from the macaroni and cheese packet, and a collection of spices to really make it come to life. For her main course, she'd use macaroni for the base of a pasta dish, bringing in a bunch of veggies and some of the soup to make a savory sauce. For dessert, she could make mini pumpkin pies using canned pumpkin, sweetened condensed milk, and the toaster pastries with coconut oil for the crust.

Piper began tossing items into her basket, and soon it was practically spilling over—mostly with elements Piper would use for her main course. She glanced at the other contestants and saw that they were toting heaping baskets, too. Jack had several cans of soup, loads of veggies, nuts, and a packet of cookies at the top of his basket. Frankie was grabbing lots of cans of fruit, freeze-dried beef Stroganoff, shortbread cookies, and olives. She had also thrown a bunch of meat sticks into her basket, and Piper cringed trying to think of what she would make with those. Not something she'd want to eat, that was for sure!

"Unfortunately," the Kitchen Wizard said, holding up a hand, "supplies are limited in this future apocalyptic world. Who's ready for today's first surprise challenge?"

The three contestants groaned.

"You may each take *eight* items from the shelter," their host said with a mischievous smile. "No more than that. You must stretch your resources if you are to have any hope of survival."

Piper looked through her basket. After a lot of thought, she selected:

A packet of crackers

A can of Italian wedding soup

Macaroni and cheese (pasta *and* cheese in one!)

Canned tomatoes

Coconut oil

Canned pumpkin

Sweetened condensed milk

Apple-flavored toaster pastries

As soon as she had her eight items, Piper returned to her workstation and laid out her meager selection of supplies. It wasn't much. But she knew if she wanted to win the $10,000, she had to make it work; even more challenging, it had to taste and look great, too.

"Your hour starts now," the Kitchen Wizard cried. "Good luck!"

Piper decided she would start with dessert, since her pies would need time to bake. She ripped open the packet of toaster pastries and attempted to scrape out as much of the apple filling as she could. She added a bit of condensed milk and coconut oil (in place of butter) to the crumbled pastry and then began forming her crust. Just as she started to whip spices and sweetened condensed milk into her pumpkin pie filling, the Kitchen Wizard and Mr. Bakshi approached and asked her some questions about her plans for the day.

"I'm working on a flatbread appetizer, followed by spicy pasta and a sauce of veggies and soup meatballs for the main dish. Then you'll enjoy a delicious mini pumpkin pie to end your meal." Piper tried to make her food sound as yummy as possible.

"Sounds very creative," Mr. Bakshi said approvingly.

"I can't wait to taste your creations," the Kitchen Wizard said, nodding brusquely.

Piper shook her head and frowned at the show's host. "I'm sorry, but I don't feed zombies."

The Kitchen Wizard and Mr. Bakshi both laughed and then moved on to Frankie's station. Piper glanced over at her competition, trying to figure out what the others were cooking. Frankie was playing around with an ice cream machine. She seemed to be crafting some sort of dessert pizza using cookies and canned fruit.

Jack was busy sautéing something in a skillet. All of a sudden, he threw his arms in the air and yelped. "No! No, no, no!"

"Everything okay over there?" Piper called as she took a taste of her pie filling.

Jack closed his eyes. Moaning, he said, "I forgot to take milk. My meal is ruined."

Piper hid a smile. For someone who had probably spent a lot of time in restaurant kitchens, he seemed to be very easily rattled. Sure, Piper had lost her cool more than a few times in the kitchen, too—but Jack seemed to have mastered the art of kitchen drama. "I have a little more condensed milk than I need," Piper told him. She glanced at the Kitchen Wizard and asked, "Are we allowed to share supplies?" One of the cameras swiveled to focus on her.

The Kitchen Wizard considered Piper's question for a minute. "I don't see why not. If you're willing to help a competitor in a time of need, feel free."

Over the past few weeks, Piper had learned a little something about giving and receiving help. She knew if she were the one in Jack's position, she would want someone to help *her*. "Take what you need," she told him. "I'm done with it."

Jack raced over and poured some of Piper's sweetened condensed milk into one of his prep bowls. "Merci beaucoup," he said, thanking her in French while blowing kisses into the air. "You are a lifesaver."

Piper finished preparing her mini pies and popped them into the oven. Then she moved on to her main dish. First she put a pot of water on the stove to boil. Next she opened the can of tomatoes. She lifted the lid and gasped when she looked inside—the tomatoes were green! She picked up the can and scanned the label—

TOMATILLOS. She had obviously misread the label earlier and grabbed tomatillos instead of tomatoes. The two looked and tasted nothing alike, except that both were round. Tomatillos were used in things like salsa verde and other Mexican dishes. "This changes things," Piper said aloud. She took a deep breath and nodded. "I can make it work."

Next she opened the soup, stirred it, and sniffed the contents. It was Italian wedding soup, which was chock-full of little meatballs, spinach, veggies, and broth. She took a spoonful and considered what—besides the tomatillos—she could add to make it taste and feel more like a sauce.

Just as she felt an idea starting to form, the Kitchen Wizard hollered, "Everyone, stop what you're doing!"

The contestants put down their tools and looked up expectantly. Piper had a feeling it was time for their second surprise challenge.

"The zombies are coming," the Kitchen Wizard droned. "The zombies are coming." All three contestants laughed as the host of the show lumbered across the set with a camera trailing behind her. In her normal voice, she went on, "As you all know, cooking is rarely a solitary pursuit. Most of the time, we cook *for* or *with* someone. This surprise challenge will test your communication and partnership skills. Imagine, if you will, that you must take refuge in a safe place, because the zombies have drawn ever closer." The lights in the studio flickered in a spooky way while the Kitchen Wizard continued her explanation. "You have no choice but to hide inside a zombie-proof pod while someone *else* finishes today's task for you. You won't be able to see your workstation, touch your equipment, or taste your food. Your only means of correspondence will be through an earpiece. You'll need to give clear-enough instructions that someone else will be able to carry out your dish in your absence."

"So we won't be the ones cooking?" Jack asked.

"Not directly, no. You will be the *brains* behind your dish," the Kitchen Wizard said, waggling her eyebrows, "but someone else will execute your orders." She held her arms out in front of herself and groaned. "Mmmm, brains."

They all laughed again.

"Who *will* be cooking?" Frankie asked.

"I was just getting to that," the Kitchen Wizard said. "This is where things get really fun. Each of you has brought friends and family from home to cheer you on during today's adventure. Before the competition began, I spoke with your cheering squads, and they helped me choose a sous-chef to join each of you in your kitchens." She waved her hand toward the wings and said, "Please welcome your zombie support team!"

14
ZOMBIE-PROOF POD

Piper and the other contestants spun around. A spotlight shone down on one side of the set. Piper couldn't wait to see who her assistant would be.

Dan? Hopefully not. (No offense to her brother!)

Her mom?

Milla?

She tried to think of whom she would *want* to cook with her and was relieved she wasn't the one who would choose.

"First up, we have Frankie's dad, Matt!" A slim man stepped out from backstage and waved at Frankie. His expression made him look like a deer caught in headlights. After studying Frankie's dad for a second, Piper noticed he also looked a little . . . strange. It took a moment for her to realize that it was because Frankie's dad had been made up to *look* like a zombie—his clothes were ripped, and his face was pasty and dead-looking. It was hilarious! Frankie raced forward and high-fived him. "Oh boy," Frankie said, laughing. "Lookin' good, Dad. This should be . . . interesting."

"Next, we have Jack's best friend and neighbor, Marguerite Elliston!" Jack sauntered over and air-kissed a tall, smiley girl who looked a little older than him. Just like Frankie's dad, Marguerite was wearing tattered clothes and rotten-looking makeup.

"Finally, please welcome Piper's friend and classmate, Mariana Sanchez!"

As soon as the Kitchen Wizard announced Mari's name, Piper was sure her family and friends had made the right choice. Mari was the only one of her friends with any real passion for cooking, and she wasn't afraid to take risks. Piper rushed forward and hugged her pal. Mari's clothes were dirty and torn, her usually tan skin was pale and crusty-looking, and her short hair was in tangles. Whether Mari was a zombie or not, Piper was thrilled to have her friend on set!

A producer yelled, "Cut!" Then there was a flurry of activity as people started talking loudly and moving set pieces around. "We need a few minutes to bring the contestants' zombie-proof pods onto the set," the Kitchen Wizard explained. "Take this time to get your partner acquainted with your workstation and explain your plans for today's task. We'll have cameras rolling in five minutes or so, and at that point you'll need to turn everything over to your zombie support team."

Piper turned to Mariana and grabbed her hands. "I'm so excited you're here with me!" she said. "When did you find out you were going to be on the show?" she asked in a rush, leading Mariana over to her workstation.

"They told us about this surprise challenge when we got here this morning!" Mari told her. "When we checked in at the front desk, a producer told us your guests had to nominate one person who would get to come on set and help you. They didn't give us any other details. Ruby suggested me, and everyone else agreed. Well, except Finley, who really wanted to do it—but your parents stepped in and said no." Mariana grinned. "My dad drove a bunch of us here, so he could sign the waiver giving me permission to participate. Then they took me backstage and gave me a zombie costume and did my makeup," Mariana said, her eyes huge. "This is *crazy*! I'm on TV!"

Both girls jumped up and down, grinning at each other. Behind them, three giant metal pods had been wheeled onto the stage. Talk about obstacles to overcome! Piper shuddered, thinking about being closed up inside that pod, unable to touch, taste, or smell her food. She obviously had no choice but to accept help during this challenge. Luckily, she had a strong partner.

"Okay, let me tell you where things stand," Piper said, knowing she had to make the most of her time with Mari. She quickly walked her friend through her supplies and equipment and explained her three courses. "I'm not sure any of this is going to turn out the way I want it to. Not because of you, obviously, just because we don't have a lot to work with. But I'm hoping for the best!"

"I love your appetizer and dessert. They sound yummy, and they're a really fun way to use the foods you had to choose from," Mari said. Then she frowned. "But can I be honest?"

"Of course," Piper said. It was nice to have someone she could bounce her ideas off.

"The pasta dish doesn't sound very exciting,"

Mariana said bluntly. "You're usually so creative, and it just doesn't seem like a very *Piper* dish. It's a little . . . boring. Is there something we could do to make it feel more *you?*"

Piper considered this. It *was* a boring dish. A safe dish. Would plain old pasta and sauce really win her the $10,000? More importantly, would she be proud to present something that didn't truly represent her creativity as a food scientist?

Mariana added, "This is your big dream, Piper. You don't want to look back later and wish you'd done more."

Piper laughed. "Correction: this is *one* of my big dreams. The food-science world better be ready for a whole lot more Piper Andelman after I'm finished here." She took a deep breath. "But you're right." She chewed her lip and considered. "I need to go out with a bang. Win or lose, I definitely want to know I went for it."

Before Piper could come up with an idea of how to make her main course bigger and bolder, a producer shouted, "Quiet on the set!"

The Kitchen Wizard stood in front of the contestants and explained, "Once the cameras are rolling, each of my three foodies will step inside one of these metal pods and be locked up. For the rest of the competition, you won't be able to see what's going on at your workstation. Your only contact with the kitchen will be through your earpiece. You'll have to rely on strong communication and trust in order to complete your dishes."

Piper grinned at Mariana. "You're going to do great," she told her. "Don't be afraid to take some risks with me, okay?"

"Got it," Mari said. "Thanks for trusting me to help you."

"We're on in five, four, three . . ." One of the producers held up two fingers, then one.

The cameras were rolling again. "Forced to take shelter from zombies," the Kitchen Wizard droned from the center of the set, "our three contestants have no choice but to direct the rest of their meal from a remote location. This will be a true test of their communication and planning skills. Contestants, please enter your zombie-proof pods."

On her command, Piper, Frankie, and Jack each stepped into their pods. There was a padded seat inside each one, but it didn't look very comfortable. Piper made a mental note to bring an extra pillow and a fluffy blanket if she ever had to hide from zombies for real.

When she slid the door closed behind her, Piper realized there was a solid metal plate blocking her view of the kitchen set. She could see out the sides of her pod, which meant she had a decent view of her fellow contestants, but she couldn't see a thing going on at her workstation. She and Mari had both been fitted with earpieces and tiny microphones—like a high-tech walkie-talkie system—that would help them communicate with each other.

"Hello?" Piper said, testing out the microphone. "Are you there, Mari?"

"Here!" Mariana said, her voice ringing in Piper's ear. "Ready for my first task, boss."

Piper giggled. This was going to be fun! "Okay, first off: Can you take a peek in the oven and see how much time is left on the pies? They might be done."

"How do I know when they're done?" Mariana asked.

"Check to see if the crusts are getting too brown. Then give the pan a little shake so you can figure out if the filling has set." Piper could hear her friend jiggling the pies inside the oven.

"The insides are still a little wobbly, and the crusts are pale," Mari reported. "Maybe five more minutes?"

Piper smiled. "Excellent instincts, chef." Next, Piper gave Mariana step-by-step instructions on her flatbread. Without tasting it, Piper couldn't figure out which spices would elevate the flavors.

She just had to trust that Mari would tell her if something didn't taste right. "Hey, Piper?" Mari asked. "What am I supposed to do with this little bowl of apple stuff on the counter?"

"Just throw it—" Piper began. But then she grinned as a better idea popped into her head. "Cheese and apple go well together, right?"

"I don't know," Mari said. "Hold on while I check." Though Piper couldn't see her, she imagined Mariana dipping a spoon into the apple toaster pastry filling, then sprinkling a bit of the powdered cheese on top. A second later, Mari reported back, "Yeah, that actually tastes really good. Kind of salty and sweet at the same time."

"Let's change it up, then!" Piper told her. She proceeded to give Mari directions for how to finish preparing the flatbread. Usually, she relied on instinct while cooking. But by having to vocalize everything, Piper found herself really thinking through her process and technique more thoroughly. It was almost like speaking her lab

notebook reports aloud!

While Mari finished preparing the flatbread, Piper took a moment to listen to what was going on with her competition. In the pod to her left, Frankie was giving orders to her dad. Though her voice was firm, she didn't sound angry or mean— just authoritative and confident. She was slowly trying to explain what "low boil" meant. Frankie looked over at Piper, shook her head, and made a funny face. She mouthed, "I'm doomed."

But then a moment later, Frankie broke into uncontrollable laughter after listening to her dad say something into the earpiece. "No, no, no," she said, closing her eyes and trying to catch her breath. "Let me explain that again." Piper loved that even in the heat of the competition, Frankie could laugh through her partner's mistakes. She hoped that after the taping was over, she and Frankie would become friends.

To Piper's right, Jack was fiddling with his hair and spinning in nervous circles inside his tiny pod. He was speaking to his best friend in a low voice, so Piper couldn't easily hear what he was saying. When he noticed Piper looking his way, he gave her a reluctant smile. "How's it going?"

Piper smiled back. "Pretty good. I'm having fun—you?"

Jack looked surprised. "Yeah," he said finally, his smile widening. "I guess I am." Even though Jack was obviously very stressed-out, he seemed like a decent guy. "Let me know if you need my help with anything, okay?" he added quietly. "I owe you for the milk. And during a zombie apocalypse, we need to take care of our neighbors, right?"

Piper nodded. "Thanks."

"Flatbread's ready," Mari said, her voice suddenly echoing loudly in Piper's ear. "What's next, boss?"

"We have to figure out what to do about my boring main dish," Piper replied, realizing she didn't have a lot of time left to play around with ideas. She thought about how talking through her worries with the Daring Dreamers Club had helped her earlier that week. Maybe if she talked through this difficulty, too, she would be able to come up with a solution. "I have some serious problems."

Just then, Mr. Bakshi appeared beside her zombie-proof pod and asked, "What kind of trouble are you having?"

After a moment's consideration, Piper decided there was no harm in telling the guest judge what she had planned. It wasn't like he could (or would) steal any of her ideas. So she quickly told him (and the cameras) about her boring pasta idea, then explained, "I like to cook, but the thing I *really* love is playing with food. It's the science and chemistry in the kitchen that I love most. I want to show you and the Kitchen Wizard my creativity, and a bowl of boring old pasta and sauce isn't going to do that. I know I can come up with something, but in such a short amount of time, it's hard!"

Mr. Bakshi nodded once. Then he said, "We have this issue in our product-development lab all the time. Often your best ideas get stuck—like a pesky can of tomatoes at the back of the pantry—and you just need to move things around a little bit to free them." He cocked his head and asked, "Why don't we look at this your way? What is the first step of the scientific method?"

"Ask a question," Piper said confidently. She often used the scientific method in her food science. She would come up with a question (the what-if of her process!), do a little research, make a prediction, and then conduct her experiment.

"Yes," Mr. Bakshi said, nodding his approval. "So let's start by asking a few questions, and we'll see if we can get your ideas unstuck."

Ruby

Who knew Piper had such a take-charge attitude? Man, watching her do her thing in the kitchen is impressive. I wonder if she's ever considered coaching as a future career? She could be a real asset on the side of the soccer field, shouting out suggestions and pointers in that no-nonsense voice of hers.

"Keira's in the middle!"

"Up the line!"

"Behind!"

Luckily, our team has a great coach (not to mention our "bonus coach": my dad, who has a habit of marching up and down the sidelines during games, yelling out his own tips from the parent section), so I guess Piper can stick with inventing and food science for now.

Speaking of my dad, my family's sort

of what I wanted to write about for the fears and obstacles journal assignment. One of the things I was most afraid of when I was little was that my parents might someday get divorced.

Then it happened.

I had no choice but to face my greatest fear, because there was nothing I could do about it. Having no control over a situation totally feels awful (which I'm sure Piper realized when she got locked up in that pod during the show). There was literally nothing I could do about my parents splitting up, and for a year or so after it all went down, life stank.

But to be honest, having divorced parents isn't as bad as I'd always imagined it would be. I know I'm one of the lucky ones, because my parents still get along pretty great. Another girl on my soccer team has parents who don't even speak to each other and can't be in the same place at the same time, and I know it's really hard for her.

My mom and dad are pretty good about not putting me and Henry in the middle when they're annoyed with each other. But it's still stressful that we have to divide our time between two different houses. And sometimes I'm a little (okay, a lot) jealous that Henry and Dad get extra time together because Dad's the head coach of Henry's soccer team. Maybe I should join Hen's team so I can have my Dad as a coach? Hmmm. Could be something to consider . . . that's probably what Mulan would do.

15
THE GOLDEN SPATULA GOES TO...

Mr. Bakshi and Mariana began firing questions at Piper. First, Mr. Bakshi asked, "What features of a dish make it interesting to you?"

Piper had no trouble answering that one. "Food that surprises you in fun ways," she said. "I love when food looks like one thing but tastes or smells like another."

Next, Mari asked, "What is one of your favorite meals you've ever created?"

"Hmmm," Piper said, pondering. Finally, she blurted out, "The first meal I got to work on from start to finish at Helping Hands. I felt like I was a part of something that really mattered."

Frankie's voice chimed in: "Which of your family members do you most love cooking for and why?"

Piper laughed. "My sister, Finley, because she likes to eat silly stuff!"

They didn't have to ask very many questions before Piper's ideas shook loose. In the course of their discussion, Piper remembered something she had read once: tomatillos have a lot of pectin. She had practiced using pectin in the animal-shaped fruit jellies she had made for her sister a few weeks earlier! Pectin was a bit like the glue of the food world. Maybe there was some way to play with that pectin and turn her main pasta dish into something more memorable. . . .

There wasn't much time, but Piper began instructing Mariana how to simmer and cook the soupy sauce, telling her to use far more tomatillos than Piper had originally planned to include. The sauce would be a little more sour than she liked, but she had a feeling she'd need a ton of tomatillos if she wanted her idea to turn out the way she was imagining it. "Here's what I'm thinking," she told Mari through her earpiece. "If we cook the sauce for the perfect amount of time, and it has time to cool a bit, we can mix the pasta and sauce together and serve it in a gelatinous mound. If this goes according to plan, the Kitchen Wizard is going to get to eat an edible pasta brain."

"Ew!" Mari said, giggling. "That sounds disgusting . . . and super fun!"

Piper agreed. This dish would be creative, it allowed her to play with science techniques, and it fit the theme of the show. It might not taste that great, and it could be a total disaster, but it was worth a shot.

Success or not, Piper knew she would have no regrets. This was a dish she would be proud to serve up as a signature Piper food-science specialty. It was time to get cooking.

★★★

When the Kitchen Wizard announced that time was up, Piper and her fellow chefs all stepped out of their zombie-proof pods. Piper raced to her workstation to see how each of her dishes had turned out. The flatbread looked good—slightly brown and crispy. Mari had executed her instructions *perfectly*. The pies looked scrumptious.

Her pasta brain, however? That was a mushy, melty, globby disaster.

"I'm sorry," Mariana said, looking devastated. "I cooked the sauce until it started to thicken, and then I put the bowl in the blast chiller to set, like you told me to. I don't know why it didn't work."

"It's not your fault," Piper said, laughing as she poked at the blobby mound of tan noodles swimming in lumpy green sauce. "I wouldn't have done anything differently myself. At least we went for it, right?" She gave Mari a big hug. "You were amazing."

All three chefs delivered their finished dishes to the Kitchen Wizard and Mr. Bakshi, who were sitting together at a long table. Slowly, the two judges tasted everything and asked the contestants a number of questions about the products they had used to construct their dishes. When the Kitchen Wizard got to Piper's noodle brains, she laughed. "Very creative," she said, "but not especially appetizing—even to this zombie."

"My brain fell apart," Piper said. "I was trying to play with the pectin in tomatillos, but something went wrong."

"To fully set," Mr. Bakshi told Piper, "pectin needs more time to cool. Your idea was inventive, and with just a bit more time it could have been brilliant. A great idea, even if it didn't work the way you'd planned."

While the two judges deliberated in front of the cameras, the contestants and their sous-chefs waited backstage. They all got to sample the other chefs' creations. Frankie's fruit pizza was beautiful but not especially tasty or exciting. And she hadn't finished her main dish; she confessed that she had cracked under the time pressure. Jack's creamy bean and vegetable stew tasted fresh and delicious, and it was almost impossible to believe he'd made it using only canned and dried food.

"This is amazing!" Piper gushed.

While everyone munched on the other contestants' dishes, Piper told them about Helping Hands. Both Jack and Frankie seemed really excited to come and help out in Duck's kitchen. "I could use some practice cooking stuff that's not cake," Frankie said.

"And I wouldn't mind getting to work in a kitchen where my dad isn't in charge," Jack said, laughing.

They made plans to all go and cook there together. Piper couldn't wait to show her new friends the ropes at her favorite place!

After they were done taste-testing, each of the chefs did one-on-one interviews where they talked about their experiences during the show. As soon as they'd finished, they were called back to the set.

The judges had made their decision.

When the cameras were rolling, the Kitchen Wizard announced, "Please help me congratulate the winner of today's challenge . . ."

Piper took a deep breath. This was it. She gazed past the lights and cameras toward her family and friends in the audience. They all waved at her, and Finley held her glittery sign high in the air.

"Jack VanDries!" The Kitchen Wizard stepped forward and presented Jack with the champion's golden spatula.

Piper and Frankie both clapped and cheered as Jack blew kisses toward the cameras. After a quick bow, he pushed Marguerite forward and urged his friend and sous-chef to take her own bow. In the front row of the audience, Arlo VanDries stood up and waved regally, acting like he was the one who had won the competition—not his son.

"Congratulations," Piper said, shaking both Jack's and Marguerite's hands. She was surprised to discover she wasn't disappointed that someone else's name had been called. After looking at and tasting all the other dishes, she and Mariana had both agreed that Jack VanDries *deserved* to win. He'd created the best dishes and executed them flawlessly.

As soon as the director hollered, "Cut," Piper's cheering section rushed to the stage. The Daring Dreamers Club enveloped her in hugs and congratulations, Duck patted her vigorously on the back, and her family beamed with pride. Everyone poked at her mushy pasta brain and gushed about her creativity and courage to make something so strange. In that moment, surrounded by friends and family who all loved and supported her, Piper knew she'd won in all the most important ways.

Of course it would have been nice to hear the Kitchen Wizard say her name, but sometime during the course of the day's competition, Piper's focus had shifted away from being crowned champion. This experience had been about so much more than $10,000 and a golden spatula. She knew she'd succeeded in the ways that mattered most to *her*—by pushing limits, taking risks, and learning something for the *next* time.

Because there was *always* a next time. And Piper couldn't wait to cook up a new adventure.

Piper

After I left <u>The Future of Food</u> set, I got emails from both Frankie and Jack reminding me about my promise to take them to Helping Hands. So a big group of us went yesterday (my family; Frankie and her family; Jack, Marguerite, and a bunch of the sous-chefs from Arlo's Bistro; and even some of Mr. Bakshi's Yum! Ice Cream food scientists!). It was <u>so much fun</u>! But the best part is that Arlo VanDries was so impressed with the facility and their mission that he donated $10,000 (the amount Jack won on <u>The Future of Food</u>) to Helping Hands! Duck hugged him so tight that Arlo might not stop by again for a while. Duck's hugs can be a little painful.

Guess what else happened? Because of my experience on <u>The Future of Food</u>, I was invited to do a molecular gastronomy segment

on the local morning news! They want me to do a weeklong series where I talk about food science and kids in the kitchen. Now that I'm a TV pro, it should be no big deal. But live TV is a whole lot different than filmed TV, and science can be a bit unpredictable . . . so I guess we'll see what happens. Frankie's offered to give me some pointers on camera-charm. ☺

So even though I didn't win the golden spatula (or the prize money), my experience on the show and everything that's happened since then has been seriously amazing. I learned a lot and had an incredible time. And you know what? This experience was just one step along the way to me achieving even bigger dreams.

In fact, I already started planning my entry for the citywide science fair, which

is coming up in a couple of months. A good
inventor knows that it's important to always
be thinking about what's next, in order to
keep life exciting!

Stay tuned, Ms. B. Because I've got a lot
more what-ifs cooking. . . .

Author's Note

Confession: I'm not a very good cook. I had to do a *lot* of research to write the cooking scenes in this story. I also enlisted the help of my kids (who love to experiment in the kitchen) and my mom and husband (who are *fabulous* cooks) to help write this story.

Piper's character was also partly inspired by the legendary American chef Julia Child, who focused on making cooking fun. Ms. Child is one of the world's most famous chefs, and is best known for making gourmet cooking accessible. She loved experimenting with food and readily accepted mistakes. She understood that the joy of cooking is more important than perfection—just like Piper. Even though—or perhaps *because*—I'm not a great cook, I love watching Ms. Child's cooking show, *The French Chef*. She had so much passion for cooking and greatly enjoyed her time in the kitchen.

As I set out to write this book, I decided that—like the Daring Dreamers—I needed to master a few cooking basics if I wanted to bring Piper and her kitchen adventures to life. A friend told me about an organization called Open Arms of Minnesota, which ultimately inspired the Helping Hands scenes in this book. Open Arms's mission is simple and true: "People who are sick should not be without food. Yet every day people in our community with life-threatening illnesses find themselves unable to shop or cook—and, often, without the support network to help." With the help of a massive volunteer network, this non-profit organization cooks and delivers free, nutritious meals to people living with life-threatening illnesses like cancer, HIV, AIDS, multiple sclerosis (MS), and ALS (Lou Gehrig's disease), as well as their caregivers and dependents.

I started volunteering to prep meals in the kitchen at Open Arms in order to give back to my community and also learn a few things about cooking tasty, healthy meals. The chefs at Open Arms are always happy to give tutorials on how to chop broccoli or beets or tell you what they're adding to their corn chowder—just like Duck and Piper do at Helping Hands. I'm so glad this book introduced me to a place like Open Arms—I get to assist people in my community while I learn how to cook. It's a win-win! I'd encourage all the readers of this series to look for someplace in your community where you can have a similar experience—a soup kitchen, food shelf, community or school food drives, homeless shelters. . . . There are a lot of places to lend a hand!

Acknowledgments

At the outset of this book, I got to sit down with food scientist Naomi Sundalius, who talked extensively about how her years of experimenting in the kitchen helped lead her to a career in food science. She explained a lot about this fascinating field, and also let me borrow a few of her ideas for this book: baking cookies using different kinds of fats, flavored-oil infusion, the concept of peanut butter in stick form for ease of baking, and the theory of using a what-if when you're working with food and science. Naomi, your help was invaluable in shaping this story. Thank you!

I'm grateful to have a helpful team of young readers who work with me on this series: Milla, Ruby, and Henry Downing, Samantha Thiegs, Frankie McConville, Stella Wedren, and Bianca Breiland. Thanks for talking all things Disney Princess with me and giving me your honest feedback on works in progress. Thanks also to

Caroline Claeson, who introduced me to the concept of advisory groups.

Cheers to my mom, Barb Soderberg, and my husband, Greg, for being incredible plotting partners—and helping with all my cooking questions!

Huge thanks to the incredible editorial, design, and brand teams at both Random House and Disney, for working to make this the best book possible: Rachel Poloski, Lauren Burniac, Michelle Nagler, Samantha McFerrin, Jean-Paul Orpinas, Megan McLaughlin, and Holly Rice. And of course, my agent, Michael Bourret, has been an amazing partner on this and every book.

Finally, thanks to Anoosha Syed for your glorious art in this series—you've really helped bring these characters to life!

DON'T MISS THE FIRST
BOOK IN THE SERIES!

MILLA TAKES CHARGE

TURN THE PAGE FOR A SNEAK PEEK . . .

Published in the United States by Random House Children's Books,
a division of Penguin Random House LLC, 1745 Broadway, New York, NY 10019,
and in Canada by Penguin Random House Canada Limited, Toronto,
in conjunction with Disney Enterprises, Inc.

Random House and the colophon are registered trademarks of
Penguin Random House LLC.

rhcbooks.com

Library of Congress Cataloging-in-Publication Data
Names: Soderberg, Erin, author.
Title: Milla takes charge / by Erin Soderberg.
pages cm — (Daring Dreamers Club ; 1)
Description: "Like Belle, Milla loves nothing more than imagining bold adventures
in the great wide somewhere. It's up to the rest of the Daring Dreamers Club—Piper,
Zahra, Mariana, and Ruby—to help Milla prove she is ready for a real grand adventure!" —Provided by publisher.
Identifiers: LCCN: 2018001619 — ISBN 978-0-7364-3924-4 (hardcover) —
ISBN 978-0-7364-3881-0 (lib. bdg.) — ISBN 978-0-7364-3882-7 (ebook)
Subjects: Adventure and adventurers—Fiction. | Camps—Fiction. | Princesses—Fiction.
| Clubs—Fiction. | Friendship—Fiction. | BISAC: JUVENILE FICTION / Media Tie-In.
Classification: LCC PZ7.S685257 Mil 2018 | DDC [Fic]—dc23

Printed in the United States of America
10 9 8 7 6 5 4 3 2 1

1
PRINCE PIGGY

"Once upon a time, in a land far, far away, there lived a handsome prince. . . ." Milla Bannister-Cook plunked down on the ground and watched as her pet pig, Chocolate Chip, trotted through the backyard. She chewed the cap of her pen and waited, hoping Chip would do something interesting so she could come up with the next line of her story. Luckily, it never took very long for Chip to spring into action.

Milla had set up the yard so it looked like a miniature fairy-tale world. Her old dollhouse was the castle, potted plants served as trees, and a family of dolls had been given the roles of humble servants. She had even placed a plastic crown on her pig's head, hoping a costume would help Chip get into character.

But that morning, Milla's prince didn't feel like playing his part. It seemed the only thing the pig wanted to do was *destroy* his land. As Milla watched, Chocolate Chip—who'd gotten his name because Milla thought his brown-and-white-spotted coloring looked like a chocolate chip cookie—began trampling shrubs and toppling flowerpots. Then he overturned the castle and pushed his royal subjects into his empty food dish.

Milla read aloud as she scribbled, "The prince in *this* fairy tale was a little different from most storybook heroes. He wasn't always graceful, he wasn't very clean, and he ate like a pig." Chip turned and grunted at Milla. She giggled, adding, "But he was sweet, strong, and extremely lovable. You just had to get to know him first. Prince

Chip's friends knew this great beast was very cuddly and always treated his family and friends like royalty. He also loved to share his beloved toys and blankets on cold nights . . . most of the time."

Chip darted across the yard when he noticed Milla pulling a banana from behind her back. He wagged his tail, waiting for the snack. "Sit," Milla told him. Chip dropped his bottom to the ground and then quickly stood up again. Milla gave her pet a firm look and repeated the command. "Sit, Chip."

But Chip was too excited about the banana to follow directions. He nuzzled Milla's shirt with his snout, spreading a muddy splotch across the front of her first-day-of-school outfit. Milla laughed, even though she knew she wasn't supposed to do that when her pig was naughty. It was important to be firm and show him who was boss, but sometimes it was very hard to hold her giggles in.

Forcing herself to frown, Milla ordered the pig to sit *again*.

Chip oinked. He butted his head up against Milla's leg. He sat, wriggled, and then let out a loud grunt. Milla could tell he was trying to prove how badly he wanted the treat. Finally, he settled his bottom on the ground and waited patiently.

"Good boy." Milla kneeled and fed him half the banana. It was gone in seconds. Chip grunted again. "Don't beg," Milla scolded, handing him the other half. "It's not polite. If you must know, you really aren't acting much like a prince." In response, Chip climbed into Milla's lap and sat down. "Oof!"

The pig settled in for a cuddle, nosing Milla for more treats. "All right, stinker," Milla said, pushing his snout away. "We'll take a break from the story. Maybe tomorrow I'll set up a cardboard city and let you be the monster that destroys it. Would you like that role better?"

Milla flopped onto her back and gazed up

at the wispy clouds drifting by overhead. Chip rested his heavy head on her stomach. "Once upon a time," she whispered, starting a new story, "there was an adventurous young girl. This brave explorer—and her pet pig—set off on a journey to the ends of the earth."

Chocolate Chip huffed a sigh.

"Yeah, yeah, I know there are no *ends* of the earth," Milla muttered. "This is just make-believe. It's not like I'm about to set off on an adventure to some far-off place anyway. Let's pretend, okay?" She continued her story. "Milla the mighty explorer and her noble pet were on a quest. They wanted to hike the tallest mountains, dogsled to the North Pole, white-water raft in the wildest rivers, and explore crumbling old castles in distant lands."

Milla loved reading and writing about anything, but there was nothing she enjoyed more than creating adventures for herself. In Milla's stories, she was always a brave hero without fears or worries of any kind. One of the things Milla most loved about writing was that she was totally in charge and got to make all the decisions about what would happen on her adventures. The only limitation was her imagination, and her imagination was vast. "Milla was the greatest explorer who had ever lived. Nothing could stop her—"

"Hon!" Milla's mom, Erica, poked her head out the back door and called, "We need to leave in five minutes or you're going to be late for your first day of fifth grade." Chocolate Chip leaped up and raced toward the house. He usually got a treat when he came inside from the backyard.

"Coming," Milla said. She brushed at her shirt, trying to wipe away some of the pig slobber and mud. Too late—it was caked on, but Milla didn't mind. She made her way toward the house, whispering, "Nothing could stop this fearless explorer . . . except for the fact that she was still just a kid and she never went anywhere other than school and her own backyard. But someday!" Milla swung her lunch up and off the kitchen counter, swiped her backpack off its hook, and headed for the front door. "Someday—*soon*— Milla the brave, bold, capable explorer would set off on her own and conquer the world."

"You'll have to conquer the world next week," Milla's other mom, Eleanor—whom Milla called mum—said in her lilting British accent. "This week's adventure is fifth grade, and school waits for no one." She pointed to a pile of folded clothes on the arm of the couch. "Get dressed, love."

Milla glanced down at the dirty shirt and jeans she was wearing. "I'm already dressed." She tugged at her dark ponytail, tucked a loose curl behind one ear, and smiled.

Milla's parents stood side by side. Her mom folded her light, freckled arms across her chest, while her mum merely raised her eyebrows. Somehow, they were both always able to say a whole lot without saying a word.

"But I like this shirt," Milla told them.

"It's covered in snout snot," her mom said. "And mud."

"It's only a *little* mud. Me and Chip's adventures are messy." Milla grinned as she pulled off her soiled shirt. She knew it was pointless to argue with either of her parents. Sassing back never seemed to work out the way she wanted it to. She wriggled into a clean pair of jeans and the bright blue cactus T-shirt her mum had set out for her. Then she waved her arms in the air. "Ta-da! Better?"

"Much," her mum agreed, leaning in for a hug. Her dark curly hair tickled Milla's cheek. "Have a great first day. I might see you after my shift tonight, if you're still awake. Yeah?"

Milla squeezed her back, breathing in the familiar smell of her mum's lemony-fresh hand lotion. Because her mum was a nurse and often worked long shifts with weird hours, Milla didn't always get to see her first thing in the morning or last thing at night. Her mom worked slightly more regular hours as a vet and usually handled most of the school pickup and drop-off duties on her way to and from the clinic.

"Chop-chop," her mom said, jingling her keys and heading for the door.

Milla slung her bag over her shoulder, then bent down to give Chocolate Chip a hug. He smelled much *less* lemony-fresh but was still lovable in his own way. The pig pressed his snout against Milla's stomach, rubbing a wet splotch right across the front of her clean shirt. She pulled away, laughing as she raced out the front door. As she fled, she called back to her mum over her shoulder, "Too late to change again. Like you said, school adventures wait for no one!"

2
First-Day Surprises

The moment her mom dropped her off in front of Walter Roy Elementary, Milla's friend Piper Andelman shouted and waved to her from across the playground. "Milla! You have to try one of these." She ran over and held out a tiny coconut-crusted muffin. When Piper smiled, her eyes sparkled behind crooked glasses. Two messy reddish braids dangled out the bottom of a fleecy winter hat. All year round, even when they were living through the hottest months of summer, Piper liked having something on her head.

"You know I can't," Milla said apologetically.

Because of her food allergies, Milla never ate any food that she couldn't be sure was safe. She'd once eaten a cookie at a preschool potluck and it had sent her to the hospital. She'd been so sick that she couldn't even remember her ride in the ambulance. Her parents were constantly paranoid about her having another reaction, but Milla had been careful about what she ate for so long now that it was second nature. "Allergies, remember?"

"Totally, one-thousand-percent nut-free. No dairy, either," Piper promised, crossing a finger over her chest. "I wiped down the whole kitchen before I made them and triple-washed every-thing. I didn't want you to have to miss out." She wiggled the muffin in midair. "I'm calling them Fifth-Grade Flurries. Coconut, carrot, a touch of cinnamon, and one little secret ingredient—a new recipe. What do you think?"

Milla took a bite, feeling grateful that her friend was always willing to work around her allergies. Coconut, carrot, and cinnamon sounded slightly odd, but somehow almost everything Piper baked or cooked tasted amazing.

Piper was part scientist, part chef, and her inventions were usually delicious. She loved playing around in the kitchen, often combining weird ingredients to create unusual new treats. Of course, there had been more than a few failures over the years: once, she'd whipped up a strange fruit punch that fizzed and bubbled like a witch's brew and turned a very yucky brown color; another time, she'd made candy that was so sticky it had yanked a filling out of one of her back teeth.

Milla popped the rest of the muffin in her mouth, trying not to gobble it up as quickly as Chocolate Chip would eat one of his treats. "That's super yummy," she told her friend. "What's the secret ingredient?"

"Soda water! I need to adjust the amount to get a little more puff next time," Piper said. "They're too flat, but still acceptable."

Suddenly, Milla felt a tug on the side of her jeans. She looked down and found Piper's little sister, Finley, gazing up at her. Finley was starting kindergarten, and Piper had been put in charge of delivering her sister from the playground to her classroom for the first few weeks of school.

"Baaaa," the little girl bleated.

"Hi, Finley," Milla said. "Are you excited for kindergarten?"

"Baaaa," Finley said again.

Piper rolled her eyes. "Ignore her. She's a naughty little sheep. I thought I lost my first-day-of-school shirt this morning—but then I figured out that Finley had stolen it. She was trying to chew *holes* in my *shirt*! This little critter claims sheep love to eat clothing."

"She's a pretty cute critter, at least," Milla said, laughing as she followed Piper and her sister off the playground and through the school's front doors. "But, Finley, isn't it goats that eat weird stuff?"

"Whatever," Piper said. "Finley's not a sheep *or* a goat, so she shouldn't be eating anything unusual. Unless I cooked it." She gently guided her sister toward the kindergarten hallway. "Fin, where's your name badge?"

Finley blinked, but said nothing more than "Baaaa" again. All kindergarteners were supposed to wear a special name badge that identified them as school newbies the entire first week. "Baaaa!" Finley shouted one last time, then galloped into her classroom.

TO BE CONTINUED . . .